THE LENORA ASSIGNMENT

THE LENORA ASSIGNMENT

By

Grey Stone

authorHOUSE®

AuthorHouse™ LLC
1663 Liberty Drive
Bloomington, IN 47403
www.authorhouse.com
Phone: 1-800-839-8640

Published by AuthorHouse   01/13/2014

ISBN: 978-1-4918-4241-6 (sc)
ISBN: 978-1-4918-4239-3 (hc)
ISBN: 978-1-4918-4240-9 (e)

Library of Congress Control Number: 2013922452

Preface

It was a special February day for Major Jack E. Abbott, USMC., when he received a phone call from the President of the United States. The President called to inform him he was to receive the Congressional Medal of Honor. It was a moment he would always remember, and he was grateful the country was acknowledging his service. However, in reality he did not feel worthy of the honor. He had seen too many of his men fall in combat. After all, they were the real heroes and the ones most deserving of the honor!

When his limousine entered the west gate of the White House, he was greeted with a brisk salute by

Colonel Samuel Gerard. He was informed he would accompany the Colonel to the Attorney General's office immediately following the ceremony. Abbott noticed, attached to Gerard's left wrist, a steel chain linked leather dossier, labeled 'Most Secret'! His mind began to race, his service record was clean and he had not intentionally violated any laws of the Geneva Convention. First things first, he was anxious to meet the President and receive his medal. At 1100 hours, the President gently placed the Medal of Honor around his neck. Within minutes following the ceremony, he and Colonel Gerard were standing before the Attorney General.

The Attorney General commissioned Abbott to clean up drug trafficking, human bondage, and prostitution. He would be known as the "Wolf", and given a license to kill. In turn, he would not report to local authorities, FBI, or CIA. His work would be clandestine and referred to as, "The Lenora Assignment". The Lenora was a sailing vessel used by large drug cartels. She sailed under the Spanish Flag and docked in her home port, Lisbon, Portugal. Let the new war begin!

Chapter 1

May 23, 2004—1600 hrs.

The container ship, 'Los Viento Buenos' left the port of Buenaventure, Colombia sailing for Los Angeles, California. She was fully loaded with various commodities, coffee beans, bananas, cut flowers, cocaine, and nine beautiful Colombian female children, ranging from eleven to sixteen years of age. The children were now in human bondage and were to become a part of a prostitution ring in Los Angeles, California.

Captain Juan Aleno had again worked his slimy deal with the Corzion family drug cartel in Buenaventure,

Colombia. The deal provided good money, while allowing him and his four crew members thirteen days at sea to molest the children!

It was not a new adventure for Juan Aleno, as a matter of fact this was his eleventh sailing trip out of the Buenaventure port to Los Angeles. His manifest always included delivery of children to Los Angeles, after which he would pick up children in Los Angeles for delivery to Seattle, Washington. A large number of the children would then be shipped via truck to Chicago, Illinois, or to New York City. Over the years his competition had been nil because he was a distant relative of Juan Corzion.

June 6, 2004—2200 hrs.

The 'Los Viento Buenos' entered the Los Angeles Harbor and was now docked at Pier #22. Captain Aleno had retired to his captain's quarters and the ships' First-mate was standing guard duty on deck. The guard watched the white passenger van pull along side the ship's mooring. The van carried the official decal markings for the City of Los Angeles, while underneath the decal the words, 'Harbor Inspection Division' appeared.

At this point the guard felt no need to notify Captain Aleno, since it appeared to be a routine port inquiry. A white male slowly opened the van door; he dropped a silver 'wolf signet', and headed for the gang-plank to board ship. The guard noticed the man wore a badge displayed on his coat lapel and he carried a small black bag over his left shoulder. Still the guard showed no cause for alarm as he extended his right hand, "Welcome aboard Senor!"

Suddenly, Abbott plunged an eight-inch knife blade into the guards' chest. The guard gasp for air and tried to scream-out but Abbott placed his left hand over the guards' mouth and lowered him to the deck.

He felt it was essential to direct his attack along the port side of the ship in order to eliminate the Captain and his crew members.

Abbott quickly moved to the hatchway leading to the Captain's quarters at midship. He planted a C-4 explosive package on the hatch-way and set the timer for ten minutes. Immediately he entered the interior of the ship and planted another C-4 package below waterline. As he moved toward the bow of the ship port side, he heard a girl scream in cargo hole # 3. When he entered the area he spotted a crew member attempting to rape what appeared to be the oldest girl. Abbott did not hesitate, he pulled his 9mm Glock from his shoulder holster and set the Laser-red beam just above the rapist right ear and fired two rounds. The shots were so accurate they literally knocked the rapist off the top of his intended victim.

Now time was of the essence, looking at his watch he had four minutes to lead the girls to safety. In just a few minutes the ship would be a burning inferno and would eventually sink in fifty-eight feet of water. As they reached the top deck two crew members opened fire with a AK 47's. Abbott and the girls didn't have time for a long drawn out fire-fight. He reached into the black bag and pulled out two concussion grenades and threw them directly in front of the two crew members. The fire-fight was over as quickly as it had started; after two large explosions the pathway to the van was cleared. As the group reached the van, the 'Los Viento Buenos' exploded and begin to sink. Within thirty minutes the nine girls were delivered to the Los Angeles General Hospital for examination and delivery to local authorities for foster care placement.

Abbott had one last thought about the Captain. Adios, Captain Juan Aleno, may your soul burn in Hell!

Chapter 2

Six months later . . . Chicago, IL.

The misty rain had stopped as Abbott entered the alley-way off North Lexington street. He was already ten minutes late for his appointment with Helen Schroeder, his good looking informant. Not only was she a smart 'cookie' but she was helpful in so many ways . . . . enough of that he thought. For now he had to keep his mind on the business at hand. That's when it happened!

He first saw the beam of the Laser red-light hit his jacket heart high ; then he heard the rifle bolt slam shut. Momentarily he froze against a gutter spout, he knew he was in deep trouble. The sniper's slug ripped through his body just below the right clavicle above the scapula causing severe pain through his shoulder. For a moment it felt like someone had stuck him with a hot poker and his right arm had been torn off. Spinning, he fell against the alley's north brick wall as his 9mm Glock landed in the middle of the alley. He would have been better off if the sniper's first round had knocked him down. Now he was a stationary target. Again he heard the sniper's rifle bolt slide another round into the chamber, somebody knew how to shoot. No time to recover the 9mm Glock since he was losing a lot of blood. Someway he had to get out of the alley, suddenly his vision became blurry and then everything turned white.

As he opened his eyes the bright lights were blinding. When he glanced to his right he saw two angels robed in white. They were really not angels, the two were RN's assigned to the Emergency Ward, Cook Hospital, Chicago. They were angels as far as he was concerned. That's when Dr. Richard Ellsworth introduced himself.

"Big fella, I'm Dr. Ellsworth and you're going to be okay. We have you stabilized now and we're going to do surgery. You have a bullet wound that needs our attention. You'll do fine."

The doctor's words were somewhat a comfort to Abbott. On numerous other occasions, he had heard those re-assuring words. He remembered hearing the words on the battlefield in 'Nam, also near that shack outside Baghdad. He felt the same now. He knew it was up to God if it be His will! That's when his vision turned white again.

Chapter 3

Dr. Ellsworth's attention was drawn to the limp muscular body lying on the operating table before him. The front upper torso reflected eight major scar tissue areas. Looking toward nurse, Clara Eddins, he asked, "Nurse, did this patient have any identification on him when you were going through pre-op procedures?"

"Yes sir, we found only a 'dog-tag' with '—USMC' printed on it."

"What's his name and dog-tag serial number?" Dr. Ellsworth inquired.

"No name or serial number, the tag reads, USMC and that's all! We did find $2600. with some small change on him and we turned the 'dog-tag' and money over to security downstairs.

Upon receipt, Officer Rhineheart called headquarters and they are sending someone out to talk to us."

Shaking his head Ellsworth said, "Let's put this man back together again!"

After three hours of intense surgery, it was time for Ellsworth and staff to leave the rest up to God, as he walked through the surgery exit doors he was met by Detective Ed Simpson, one of Chicago's finest.

"Dr. Ellsworth, may I have a word with you?", asked Simpson.

"Yes, how may I assist you?"

"Doctor, I'm Detective Ed Simpson, Chicago Homicide Division. I understand you have a patient who has received a gunshot wound. Is that correct?"

"Yes, we just finished major surgery on him. Follow me to the ICU waiting area and I'll brief you.

"First of all, we have a white male, approximately fifty two—to fifty five years of age who appears to be in excellent physical condition with the exception of the bullet wound, which really tore up his right shoulder. He's lost a lot of blood through external bleeding. Presently, we have him in stable condition; however, we'll hold him in ICU for a couple of days so we may monitor him on a twenty-four hour basis."

Simpson replied, "I checked with security when I came up but Officer Rhinehart was out of pocket. Can you give me ID information concerning your patient?"

"No, I'm afraid we're a little short on ID information. The nurses gave all the info they had to Officer Rhinehart."

"All I can tell you about this individual is that he has taken care of himself, and from the body evidence he has been in one hell of a fight! I've never seen as much scar tissue on a living human being. For a fact, somebody, somewhere in times past, have apparently tried to cut him in half with a high caliber weapon."

"When will I be able to talk with him?"

"Let's give the big guy twenty-four hours. It would be best if you would call nurse Eddins and set an appointment time for interview. She'll let me know so I can be on hand. I don't want to lose this one. I'll tell you for a fact, he is one tough hombre." With the closing remark, Dr. Ellsworth excused himself and headed down the hall to visit other patients.

Detective Simpson recognized he had a lot of work to do, including finding Officer Rhineheart and secure whatever evidence hospital security had to offer. After which, he would visit the ambush scene off north Lexington Street.

Chapter 4

The rain had set in again, aided by a slight breeze from the north. Just enough to be chilly in the windy city. As Simpson entered his apartment it was time to relax, have a beer, with a cold baloney sandwich and watch the ten pm. news. Since the homicide division had placed a 'gag' order on the shooting there would be no mention of the incident on any of the news channels.

After Simpson turned off the television set, he could hear the traffic outside with an occasional horn blasting away. His apartment house, The Stoneleigh, was located on NW Douglas Drive and normally was very quiet in the evening hours; however; tonight it seemed to be an extremely busy place and just a little nerve-racking. Maybe it was because he was still uptight thinking about the dog-tag, USMC without Name, MOS or Serial Number!

He was restless, tossing and turning at 0210 hours he awoke and was not able to go back to sleep. Sensing it was a hopeless situation he thought maybe a fresh cup of coffee would settle his nerves and he would be able to rethink the previous day's activity. After finishing the second cup of freshly ground coffee, he thought of a lead he had overlooked. He needed to visit with his friend, Howard Long, dispatcher for the Metro Ambulance Service division. Hurriedly he got dressed and headed for the Metro Emergency Ambulance Services office, located downtown Chicago. Upon arrival he was greeted by Sergeant Hartsell, the dispatcher a long time friend.

Smiling, Hartsell said, "Good morning, 'gum-shoe', what brings you out this early morning? I thought detectives retired at six pm. and came to work about noon the next day."

Simpson replied with a slight frown on his face, "Hartsell, I thought by now you would have grown-up and learned to respect the law enforcement division. If I had known you were on duty I would have waited until noon!"

"When does my friend Howard come on duty?"

"Simpson, you've just got me. Mr. Howard Long is on vacation."

Both men smiled and shook hands. Since they had not seen each other in three years, they briefly reminisced about having previously worked a case together.

Hartsell asked. "How can I help you this morning?"

"We had a shooting victim delivered to Cook Hospital by one of your units. I need to visit with your driver and medics in attendance during the pick-up and delivery."

With a inquisitive look, Hartsell asked. "What time are we talking about?"

"I'd estimate sometime around 1900 hours . . . . off Lexington Street!"

"Simpson, Lexington is a damn long street. North or South Lexington?"

"Hartsell, have you ever thought of becoming a detective? You sure as hell ask a lot of detail questions. It was in the three hundred block off North Lexington about a hundred yards in the alleyway. The victim was moving from east to west in the alley when a sniper downed him. I believe the victim has type 'A' blood.

"Would you please give me your unit number and the driver's name who made the pickup. I need to talk to him or her as soon as possible."

Smiling, Hartsell replied. "No need to get testy. Our ambulance services are divided into zones and I just needed to determine which zone the pickup was made."

With a bewildered look, Simpson said, "Okay, Hartsell, my fault. I'm a little up tight on this one and I haven't slept well. We've got a very unusual case as the victim has little identification and I'm grasping for straws."

Hartsell examined his ambulance assignment sheets. "Yep, that was unit #54 and the driver was Claudia Hefner, she was assisted by Larry Covington and Sid Young. Now, let me check the report sheet. Here we go, yeah, they picked up your man and initially thought they had a corpse! I'll make you a copy of their report . . . maybe this will assist you."

Quickly glancing over the delivery report Simpson noticed, Hefner and Covington had turned in a small piece of blood stained paper, plus a small silver signet with a Wolf's face imprinted on the surface. Apparently the items had fallen out of the victims jacket when he was being loaded onto the stretcher. For safe keeping the items were turned in to Metro's security claims office.

"Hartsell, sorry to bother you again but I need one more favor."

Smiling again, Hartsell said. "Sure thing, but I'm not buying you breakfast!

What else do you need?"

"This report indicates you have a couple of items found on the victim when they delivered him to Cook Hospital. I would like to have those items for my investigation.

"My friend, you shall have same," replied Hartsell.

As Simpson received the small piece of blood stained paper and the silver Wolf signet, he noticed smeared writing on the paper. The writing was not legible with the naked eye, so he quickly bagged the evidence and headed for police headquarters.

Chapter 5

0453 hours.

Marty Stewart was working the front desk. "Well, as I live and breath here comes, Simpson, my favorite detective. Did your lady friend throw you out this early? She's either ill physically or she's lost her marbles, whatever! You don't look so good! What's happening?"

"Marty, I need your help. Please pull up all computer data we have on the local Marine activities within the last year and contact Marine Headquarters, Quantico, Virginia. We need assistance in identifying an individual who's wearing a 'dog-tag' showing USMC with no name, mos or serial number.

About all we have is a live body lying in ICU at Cook Hospital.

"We will forward what DNA we have within the next twenty-four hours.

"I have a couple of items I need to project on the big screen so I'll be in the conference room if you need me."

"For you, anything! By the way, the Chief doesn't want you projecting any porno stuff. Do you understand me?"

Smiling, Simpson called out. "Dearest Marty, I wouldn't dare do it without you."

Cook Hospital, 0605 hours. Shift change.

Helen Schroeder, alias, Ann Duvall presented her fake CIA identification badge and card to the nurse on duty in the ICU. Duvall instructed her, Agent Andrew Scoggins was to be moved to a military care unit immediately because of security reasons. The nurse responded by telling Duvall she would have to have Doctor James Barnett's approval. She immediately left her work station to locate the doctor. Due to the shift change causing some state of disorder and lack of immediate assigned responsibilities among the hospital staff, it was an excellent time for Duvall to activate the fire alarm system. Within ten minutes she had managed to clear the ICU and hospital grounds with the hospital's mystery patient, Andrew Scoggins now in her care and keep.

Simpson's viewing through overhead projection had produced satisfactory viewing. The small parcel of paper was from an embossed envelope showing a return address for International Oil and Gas Exploration Company on South Colorado Blvd., Denver, Colorado. The 'Wolf' silver signet piece had no stamping marks; however the engraving was of good quality.

First things first, he made photo's then delivered the items to his forensic unit for further evaluation.

After making a stop at Mel's diner and enjoying a well rounded breakfast, it was time to go to work. He vividly remembered Dr. Ellsworth instructing him to call head nurse, Clara Eddins to setup an appointment before he attempted to visit the man with the unusual 'dog-tag USMC.' Since it was nearing O900 hours it would be a good time to make the phone call and set the appointment time.

When he entered police headquarters he was told to report to Captain Turner's office immediately. Walking into Captain Turner's office, the air was fresh and clear, Turner had not lit one of his infamous cigars as yet; he greeted the captain with a smile.

"Good morning sir, I understand you wanted to see me upon my arrival."

"That's right Simpson, I'd like to say good morning to you; however I'm not sure it would be a truthful statement!"

"Captain, what's up?"

"I'm afraid we've lost the shooting victim you were trying to identify."

"What are you talking about? Has he expired?"

"Nope, the man just vanished!"

"Vanished, how could he? The man was near death shortly after he was shot."

Frowning, Captain Turner said. "You'd better get over to Cook Hospital and get all the details. I'm not sure about anything anymore."

Chapter 6

Helen Schroeder possessed fair skin, chiseled facial features, with green penetrating eyes, and auburn hair cut to shoulder length. She stood 5'8" in flats and maintained a well formed body. Back in her prime she was a beauty and still had a lot to offer. She had previously served as an FBI Agent in New York, San Francisco, and Los Angeles, California. During her service years she had received special training in karate, hand to hand combat, including knife and stick fighting. In addition, she was an expert in small arms weaponry, bomb and booby trap manufacturing. After 20 years of FBI service she knew the street and how to survive. Over the years she had developed numerous personal contacts which were beneficial to her in her new profession as a . . . informant!

Her change of occupation was always a concern to those who had worked with her and knew her best. In Los Angeles she had lost her last partner, Steve Hightower in a support raid with the Treasury Department. If only Steve would have allowed her to take the 'lead' as they entered the warehouse, he would still be alive. Many rumors indicated she and Steve were lovers, only rumors! Suddenly she retired from the FBI.

Helen's current place of abode was not much to write home about. There were two factors which dictated her place of residency. First, price, the second location; however the place had to be clean and in a drug free neighborhood.

Presently, she would share her duplex flat with her friend and confidant, Jack Abbott, alias, Andrew Scoggins. The duplex was located on south Jefferson street about a block south of Lexington. The first floor of the flat was comfortable, with living room, bedroom, kitchen, bath and utility room. For now Jack could sleep in the bedroom and she'd take the couch in the living room. She had given special emphasis to security of the flat, especially the basement. The basement was important since it was somewhat of a war-room. It was utilized as a gym for workouts, small arms arsenal, and lab for shaping C-4 explosive charges and detonators.

The area was well ventilated for storing a small supply of cyclotrimethylene trinitramine, dioctyl sebacate. The small arms inventory was very adequate to start a good fire-fight!

After dressing Jack's wounded shoulder and pulling up his bed covers, she begin to reminisce about their meeting. It was 2003 when she and Steve Hightower stopped-in at the Whaler's Bar and Grill located in east Los Angeles. She was introduced by a mutual friend and informant, Dave Snider. Helen, and Steve had previous dealings with Snider. On this evening she and Jack became friends. As the years past they stayed in touch via email and phone.

Sometime they would assist each other on special assignments. Helen was familiar with Jack's operation and was about to relate valuable information when the sniper intervened. She would provide nursing care and security for Jack until he regained his health. If need be she would be willing to carry out his assignment.

When she retired for the evening Helen tossed and turned finding it difficult to sleep.

First she thought it might be due to the shortness of the couch, then she realized it was due to the pressure of current events. How did the sniper find Abbott? Did he or she know about his scheduled meeting and his destination? One big question would remain unanswered. Did the sniper know about her and the relationship she has with Abbott?

Come morning she would share the information she had obtained for Abbott. For a moment Helen's mind centered on the nine young girls from Columbia who were now in the Los Angeles area recovering from a horrible journey. Thanks to, Jack Abbott, USMC, aka, the Wolf, they would have a chance at a new start in life. At this point she realized she must help Jack regain his health.

Chapter 7

Simpson arrived at Cook General and headed for the Administration Office.

As he produced his credentials he glanced toward the conference room and saw Dr. Ellsworth, head nurse of ICU, Clara Eddins and officer Rhinehart seated at the conference table with three other people. Ellsworth looked up and motioned for him to join the group. With a faint smile, Ellsworth greeted him. "Good morning, detective. We were about to call your office. I'm confident you know by now our special patient has checked out of this hospital!"

"Yes sir, I got the word. Are you at the point you can give me details?"

The hospital administrator spoke up, "Yes my secretary, Mrs. Bennett seated to my left has taken notes of this meeting and will furnish you a written report."

Looking left, Simpson acknowledged, Mrs. Bennett's presence by nodding. Dr. Ellsworth continued his conversation, "Detective Simpson, it appears we have been had. A woman posing as CIA agent, Duvall snookered our staff, then set off the fire alarm system. The woman identified the patient as, Agent Andrew Scoggins and implied the quick 'check-out' had to do with security measures!"

Simpson responded, "Dr. Ellsworth, I'm not too sure the woman did not make a true and accurate statement in part. I personally believe we have a very unusual situation developing. We currently have some DNA samples our lab is checking out. By the way, we would appreciate any additional DNA your hospital may furnish."

Shaking his head in agreement, Ellsworth said, "Absolutely, no problem. Is there any other way we may assist you?"

"Yes, I would like to interview the nurse on duty at the time Duvall and Scoggins pulled the disappearing act; maybe officer Rhinehart can set-in the meeting and help fill in some gaps."

Rhinehart remarked, "I'll be happy to participate. I know for sure when the fire alarm sounded everything seemed to go to hell in a hand-basket!"

Looking directly at the hospital administrator, Simpson asked. "When may I have the written report?"

"Mrs. Bennett, will furnish you the report as you are interviewing the duty nurse in ICU."

The meeting was adjourned and Simpson and Rhinehart headed for ICU.

While on the elevator, Simpson asked, "Rhinehart, what's your evaluation of this situation?"

Shaking his head from side to side, "Simpson, I have to admit I'm really messed up on this one. I've been stationed at this hospital for seven years and I've seen some strange things happen but nothing like this."

As they reached the second floor they stopped at the ICU waiting room.

"Well, I'll have to admit it is a little mind boggling. Let's take a break before we visit with the 'on duty' nurse. Tell me everything you know about the man who was brought in here with a gun shot wound"

Leaning over closer to Simpson, Rhinehart spoke softly. "When this 'Scoggins' fella was delivered to the emergency ward he was soaked in blood. As the nursing staff prepared for surgery they gave me twenty-six hundred dollars plus eighty cents in change. That amount is still locked in the hospital's security safe.

"I did not have an opportunity to really check 'Scoggins' out. I could tell he was a middle aged man, with fair complexion and dark brown hair. He had good facial features I'd guess he weighed somewhere around two-hundred pounds and was at least six feet in height. It was kinda hard to measure since he was on a stretcher."

With an inquisitive look, Simpson asked. "Since you have been talking with hospital personnel have you heard any conversation which would assist us in truly identifying this individual?"

With a faint smile, Rhinehart replied. "The only names I've heard mentioned are Ann Duvall and Andrew Scoggins. I guess both of those names are fraudulent."

Simpson answered. "I believe you're right in your assessment."

As usual the hospital was a busy place as Simpson and Rhinehart approached the nurses station. They were greeted by RN Nancy Riggins.

"Good morning, Rhinehart. How may I assist you guys today? Riggins asked.

"And a good morning to you Nancy. I would like you to meet Detective Simpson. He needs to ask you questions regarding the Scoggins fella. May we go to your office where there's not so much noise?"

"Sure, I think it best." She quickly glanced toward Simpson, "It's good to meet you detective, I'll try to help anyway I can."

"Mrs. Riggins, I do appreciate your time today. We've got a tough case on our hands. Please tell me about your meeting with Ann Duvall."

At that moment Dr. James Barnett stepped to the office door and introduced himself.

Smiling, he asked, "May I be of help in someway?"

"It's good to meet you Dr. Barnett, Simpson replied. You are certainly welcome to join our meeting. I understand you were on duty when, Mr. Scoggins abruptly checked out of Cook Hospital without your approval."

"That is correct, Mrs. Riggins had sought my assistance whenever the CIA agent told her that.

Nancy Riggins suddenly stood up. "I'm sorry please excuse my manners. Would you gentlemen care for a cup of coffee.? I think I could use a cup to settle my nerves."

Rhinehart responded, "That sounds good." Mrs. Riggins left the room immediately.

It was a good time to take a break and it gave Simpson an opportunity to become better acquainted with Dr. Barnett.

Dr. Barnett continued the conversation. "Gentlemen, I felt it best to join your meeting.

Mrs. Riggins has been so nervous and upset over this incident."

Simpson, looked directly at Barnett. "Doctor did you check on Scoggins during your morning rounds?"

"Yes, I said good morning to the patient and checked his medical charts."

"Did he respond to you when you said good morning?".

"Yes the patient responded by saying he felt much better. His medical charts were in good order and reflected all of his vital signs were good."

"Did you examine the patient's wound and other parts of his body?"

"I did, and directed the nurse to treat the wound and to change the bandage wrappings."

"Did you notice any particular markings on his body, like serial numbers or any other features which would help identify this man?"

Frowning, Dr. Barnett answered, "No numbers or tattoos, only heavy scar tissue.

I determined the patient had been in the military and had suffered numerous wounds or he had met somebody who didn't like him very much."

"Doctor, did you have the privilege of meeting Ann Duvall during this period?"

"No sir, Mrs. Riggins will have to fill you in on that one."

Just as Dr. Barnett finished his statement Nancy Riggins returned to her office with four cups of fresh brewed coffee.

"Sorry, it took me so long. For some reason our staff is not too attentive in making fresh coffee when they are staring at an empty coffee pot."

Simpson responded, "Not to worry, Mrs. Riggins, it seems this type behavior is common in most business places."

Dr. Barnett said, "Nancy, in your absence I've given Detective Simpson my statement relating all I know about, Ann Duvall and Scoggins. I'm afraid I have not been much help."

"On the contrary, doctor your input tells us our Mr. Scoggins is a fast healer. The fact he was able to leave the hospital confirms your report. Thanks for the information. If you think of anything else which would help locate this individual please give our headquarters a call."

Doctor Barnett acknowledged Simpson's request with a friendly nod and excused himself from the meeting. Simpson turned his attention to Mrs. Riggins.

"Mrs. Riggins, I want to thank you for your hospitality this morning. Please be relaxed as I ask you a few questions, okay?"

"Detective Simpson, I feel I have really messed up since I left my duty station.

Ann Duvall made me really nervous. I guess when she introduced herself as a CIA agent.

It seemed so real and over my head, I felt I needed immediate assistance. That's the reason I hurried to find Dr. Barnett. I rely on him a lot since we usually work the same shifts."

With a faint smile, Simpson replied, "Mrs. Riggins, I feel you followed Cook General Hospital's protocol. I can see why you would react the way you did. It's not everyday a professional person such as yourself would have dealings with a CIA or FBI agent. These folks you were dealing with are professionals. They knew what to do and how to do it! Now, let's talk about the so called, Ann Duvall. What can you tell me about her?"

With her voice quivering, "She was an attractive lady, I'd say she was probably in her mid-thirties, well dressed in a black business suit and carried a large black bag. I think it had some kind of a government emblem on the side, like Central Intelligence Agency or something like that. I'm really not sure! Her voice was pleasant but very firm and business like. She introduced herself and presented identification which seemed to be authentic.

Then she said, We're moving Agent Scoggins to a military facility due to security issues."

"You are sure she said, Agent Scoggins?"

"Yes sir, absolutely sure. She said Agent Andrew Scoggins."

"Interesting," Simpson commented.

"That's when I told her I would have to secure the Doctor's approval and I went to find Dr. Barnett. When I returned with the doctor, both she and the patient were gone. A lot was happening about this time since the fire alarm had sounded."

"Prior to Ann Duvall's arrival had you visited the patient?" Simpson asked.

"Yes, I was with Dr. Barnett as he visited each patient in the ICU that morning."

"Did the hospital staff ever visit the patient to gain additional information to obtain identification?"

"No sir, the administration staff would have conducted that inquiry later on in the day. All of this was going on much earlier just as shift change was being made."

"At this point can you remember anything else happening as far as Duvall or Scoggins are concerned?" Simpson asked, as he closed his pocket notebook.

Somewhat relieved, Mrs. Riggins said, "Oh, one other thing. One of our housekeeping employees found this item in Scoggin's cloths closet. It must have dropped out of his street clothes." Mrs Riggins handed Simpson a small silver signet of a wolf!

Chapter 8

Three weeks of rehabilitation had been good for Jack Abbott. Certainly, Helen Schroeder had shown tender loving care to help mend the shoulder wound and to lift Abbott's spirit! The time had been well used by both parties. Helen had time to modify a new Glock 9mm, with fake serial number, new barrel and a new firing pin, plus prepare an adequate amount of C-4 compound. In Jack's line of work her modifications were essential and the new compound would help out and hopefully assure his continued success.

On the other hand Jack had been thinking about the assassin who put him down. He was confident someone knew of his whereabouts and his relationship with Schroeder. It was time for him to move on.

"Helen, it's time for me to go. I want to thank you for the nursing care and special attention you have given me. I owe you a lot and your kindness and thoughtfulness will always be remembered. It's obvious the assassin knew I was to rendezvous with somebody, I'm not sure he or she knew it was with you. For this reason please stay alert, because I care about you." He slowly pulled Helen close and kissed her goodbye.

"Jack, where are you going?"

"It's best you do not know, I'll be in touch!"

Placing the rebuilt Glock 9mm in his shoulder holster, he smiled as he swung the black bag of C-4 compound over his right shoulder. Walking down the driveway he turned south as he reached Jefferson Street and he was soon out of sight.

It was 0500 hours when Schroeder picked up her copy of Chicago Tribune Newspaper.

She could not help but notice the headlines, The Angels Club on Hubbard Street was completely destroyed by a well placed bomb, killing the proprietor, Jake Lamons and three male members of his staff. The article continued by stating, twenty-eight female prostitutes had been picked-up and delivered to Cook General Hospital for examination and rehabilitation.

As she finished her second cup of coffee the phone rang, when she placed the receiver to her ear she heard a familiar voice. "Good morning, nurse Duval,"

"You nut! I see you have been hard at work."

"Yep, had a little extra time on my hands so I decided to put it to good use. By the way, the young ladies referenced in the article were from Peru!"

"Let us pray their lives will find meaning in the days ahead. Where are you now?"

"Near the railroad tracks. Have you heard from anyone of importance, like maybe Dave Snider?"

"No, not a word, will you be coming to see me?"

"Not this time, you take care of yourself. I'll be in contact in a couple of weeks."

The phone line became open with the familiar dial tone. The wolf was gone.

Chapter 9

Approaching Police Headquarters, Detective Simpson was still having difficulty putting the puzzle together. At this point he had very little information to go on. Reviewing the events which had occurred within the last three and a half weeks, he thought he would have Mr. Scoggins or Ann Duval located by now. Too many parts of the puzzle were missing, his inquiry to the United States Marine Corp had not been acknowledged. The DNA samples from Cook Hospital had been misplaced. All he had to go on was the blood stained envelope showing the Denver Colorado address of International Oil and Gas and the small silver wolf signet.

When he walked through the front doors of Police Headquarters all seemed to be as usual. He greeted, Sergeant Griffin the booking officer of the day who had two prostitutes, one peeping tom, and two teenagers standing in line to be booked. Both teenagers needed a bath real bad.

Making his way back to his office he smelled cigar smoke coming from Captain Turner's office. Apparently, Turner had just lit one of his cigars he claimed came directly from Cuba. He would often say some of the cigars had Fidel Castro's finger prints on the cigar bands.

The entire police unit knew better; however it didn't hurt to stroke the captain's ego ever now and then.

While Simpson was checking his email and telephone messages, Captain Turner walked into his office puffing on the cigar. For a moment you would have thought Coal Train #99 had just rounded the bend as the smoke curled around Turner's head.

"Okay Simpson, what have you got on the fellow who was shot near Lexington Street?"

"Chief, the information I've been able to glean is really skimpy. The only leads I have are a partial blood stained envelope, showing a business address in Denver, Colorado plus a small silver wolf signet."

"Let me see the wolf, hmm good engraving job! Have you brought the Denver group into this case?"

"No sir, my personal feeling is we're dealing with a CIA agent or FBI agent, maybe both and it would be best for us to row our own boat for awhile."

"Simpson, you have one helluva imagination or you have some reason for saying that, which is it?"

"The modus operandi used when the so called, Ann Duval checked the so-called, Mr. Scoggins out of Cook General Hospital. In my opinion these folks are not playing games, we are dealing with professionals. During the check-out process, Duval used the term, Agent Scoggins! There's a possibility the 'The Angel Club' bombing last night and the demise of Lamon's gang is tied in someway to our case. If so, it's just the beginning and we had better order some more body bags!"

"Well, somebody should have done Lamon in long ago. Do you feel Scoggins did it?"

"Chief, if the bomb squad confirms C-4 was used then I would say he's our man."

"Tell me, have you linked up with the FBI or CIA on the Lamon case?"

"No sir, I have not contacted their local offices; nor have I heard a peep from them.

All of us seem to be going our separate way, that's another reason I believe this case may be National or International in scope! Chief, I know your busy, what's the chance of having dinner with me tonight, so we may have some quality time to discuss this case. I'll even spring for dinner and a couple of drinks at the Sheraton. Are you available?"

Quick, came the Captain's reply, "Simpson, I can't remember the last time I passed up free drinks and a good dinner. I'll meet you at the Sheraton at 1900 hours sharp."

The Sheraton's dining room was an ideal place to promote Simpson's cause.

"Chief, I need to go to Denver, Colorado!"

Chief smiling, "Well, I should have known the free drinks and dinner was not going to be free, 'nothing is free anymore', just joking, Simpson. I know you've got your teeth in this 'Scoggins' case and I don't blame you. How long are we talking about and how much is it going to cost my department?"

"I'm thinking a week to ten days at a cost of a grand!"

"Now, you've already had your vacation, right?"

"Yes sir, I spent a week in Aspen, Colorado about two months ago."

"Alright, drop by my office tomorrow about 1400 hours and I'll have you a cash advance ready. By the way, if you don't have something concrete for me to show the Mayor upon your return, your ass will be mine, understood?"

"Yes sir, you've made your point very clear."

"Now, where are the girls for this evening?"

"Chief, I'm fresh out. You've been working me so hard I just haven't had time to think about women!"

"Yeah, I had forgotten about you being a workaholic. Let's get out of this money making place. I guess I'll have to be content to watch one of the late shows or a cable news channel, Simpson, you're not fun anymore!"

Chapter 10

It was 2100 hours when Simpson's Frontier's Flight touched down at Denver International Airport. The flight was enjoyable except for the passenger seated next to him. Seems the man knew all the Denver Bronco's by first name, previous injuries, potential and blood types! Simpson didn't feel it best to talk in depth about his Chicago Bears or the whole NFL might be reviewed.

Finally after a thirty-minute delay in deplaning he had a rental car and was on his way to the hotel located on South Colorado Blvd. If his map reading was correct he would be only a few short blocks from the International Oil and Gas Corporation's office.

As he retired for the evening he could not help but think of 'Scoggins and Duval', and he felt somewhat ill at ease not knowing their real names. He knew for a fact his trip to the Denver area was a long-shot at best. Hopefully, the folks at International Oil and Gas would be able to steer him in the right direction.

When morning came Simpson woke up craving a big breakfast, maybe like his favorite menu of ham and eggs, with hot biscuits, apple butter and continuous serving of hot coffee.

As Simpson approached the hotel desk clerk he could not help but notice the two seater couch situated in the lobby, facing the clerk's counter. It was not so much the couch that caught his attention but the attractive blonde, with the black pen-stripped dress suit and the stiletto high heels which caused him to take a second look. Looking at the hotel clerk, Simpson asked. "Pardon me, could you recommend a nearby restaurant?"

"Sure can, you'll find the Alpine Restaurant three blocks down on the west side of the boulevard. They have an excellent breakfast menu."

"Thanks a lot." As Simpson moved toward the front doors he glanced back toward the couch. The attractive blonde still had her head buried in the local paper, The Denver Herald.

When Simpson walked into the Alpine Restaurant he felt the hotel clerk really knew what he was talking about. The place was like a bee hive, fortunately there was a vacant booth and table nearby. The hostess was quick to usher him to the booth and furnish him a menu.

He was about to order when the attractive blonde walked in and was seated at the empty table.

Some folks would refer to her as being 'good-looking', others might say she was 'a keeper.' In his mind either one would fit the occasion. The lady was 5' 8", brown eyes, and the hair was well coiffured, and her body was slender and well shaped. When she looked up, she lay aside the menu and gave Simpson a 'Mona Lisa' smile. That did it!

"Pardon me, I noticed you in the hotel lobby. Since I hate to eat alone, will you join me for breakfast?"

"I too dislike eating alone. I'll be happy to join you provided we go 'dutch treat'."

"Great! I'm, Ed Simpson from Chicago. And you are?"

"Kathy McBride, from New York."

"Kathy, you are a long way from home, what brings you to this beautiful city?"

"I'm with the Paramount Modeling Agency and I'm here on business. What about you, why Denver?"

"I'm here negotiating with a major oil and gas company."

Turning her head to the side with somewhat of an inquisitive look, "You know the oil and gas business has always been fascinating to me. While you are in the Denver area maybe you could teach me the 'in's and out's' of the business."

"Truly, it will be my pleasure," replied Simpson.

As the two new acquaintances continued breakfast they established the fact, both were single, mature adults with no other special persons involved. Suddenly, Kathy was standing, "Ed, I'm sorry I must rush if I'm to make my appointment." She leaned over the table and laid ten dollars down. I believe that will cover my part. I'm registered at your hotel. Please give me a call about 8:00 pm. and we'll meet at the hotel bar."

The Page Office Building on South Colorado boulevard was a eleven story office building with well manicured lawn and shrubs surrounding the building. As

Detective Simpson walked in the granite lobby he notice the office marquee located near the flowing fountain in the center of the lobby. A quick glance indicated International Oil and Gas was located on the fourth floor, room 416. Stepping off the elevator he turned right down the hallway, he encountered a well dressed man with a friendly smile.

"Good morning," came a warm greeting. May I help you in someway?"

Simpson was somewhat surprised by the early morning greeting. "Yes, I'm trying to locate, Andrew Scoggins. Do you happen to know him?"

"No sir, did you check with the office manager down stairs?"

"No, I didn't. I believe he works for International Oil and Gas, Room 416."

The stranger replied, "Well, good luck on that one. Those folks seem to be always out of town. I've never met, Mr. Scoggins. I do know the postman sometimes leaves packages with our building superintendent, James Ivey. You might want to check with him, he may be able to help you."

"Thanks, I appreciate your help," replied Simpson.

Soon the stranger was out of sight and Simpson continued his journey until he reached Room 416. Knocking on the door without any response, he glanced through the door mail drop and saw several envelopes laying on the floor. A smart detective knew this was not a good sign.

It was time to visit with the building superintendent, James Ivey. When he reached the superintendent's office, it seemed all hell had broken loose. A great deal of cussing was going on, with frequent words murdering the King's language.

Mrs. Arlene Biggers had just reported the girl's toilets on the second floor were flooding. For sure Simpson knew the 'super' would not be in a good mood when approached. Somehow, he would have to engage him in conversation. At all cost, Simpson needed to enter the offices of International Oil and Gas!

After the conversation with, Mrs. Biggers had calmed down, Simpson knocked on the door.

"Just a minute," Ivey replied. He opened the door and apparently regained his composure.

He greeted Simpson with a smile, "Yes sir, come on in. How may I assist you?"

"Hope I'm not interrupting," Simpson responded.

"No, not at all. I've got to call the plumbing company. We've got a problem on the second floor, nothing we can't handle. What's on your mind?" Arlen Biggers excused herself and left the office huffing and puffing!

"I'm Ed Simpson, Detective from Chicago. I'm here to contact a member of International Oil and Gas. Simpson suddenly felt the need to show his credentials.

"I'm trying to locate, Mr. Andrew Scoggins with the International Oil and Gas, do you happen to know him?"

Smiling, Ivey replied, "Not really, I've received some of the packages mailed to him from the Chicago area; but I've never seen him. Is he in trouble?"

"No sir. He's been missing for sometime and we're concerned about his good health.

I'd appreciate if you would allow me in his office to check the mail that's been deposited on the office floor. Would you do that for me?"

"Oh hell, I'd like to know more about him myself. You being an officer of the law, I guess it would be alright. Do you need a search warrant?"

Simpson smiling, "Not if it's just between you and me. Here's a hundred bucks for your time."

"Follow me," Ivey answered.

Entering the corporate offices of International Oil and Gas, Simpson could tell the office had not been used for some time. Dust covered the office equipment and the window blinds were drawn shut. Ivey was the first to enter and he warned Simpson to watch his step as numerous pieces of mail were scattered on the floor in line with the mail drop. Apparently the answering machine was still on and the receiving light was blinking. Ivey immediately pushed the answering button. They heard the following message.

"Good morning, this is, Ann Duval, you have reached the Corporate Offices of International Oil and Gas. Please leave a message and Mr. Scoggins will return your call as soon as possible."

Ivey picked up the loose mail on the floor and stacked it neatly on the desk. "Duval needs to check-in more often," He commented.

Simpson picked up on the remark in a hurry. "Oh, do you know Ann Duval?"

"Yep, sure do, she is one sexy woman. She usually shows up about every couple of months. I know for a fact, she gets a lot of attention from the men in this building when she enters the building or walks down the hall." Ivey continued to describe Duval and his description matched the one given by the employees at Cook Hospital in Chicago.

As Simpson continued to glance around the office, he noticed various military pictures decorated three walls. The famous Iwo Jima flag raising picture was huge, along with several pictures of Corsair Fighter Aircraft and four F106's were depicted in flying formation. When he neared the desk, he asked Ivey for permission to look at the envelopes he had placed on the desk.

Ivey did not answer but he did nod his head up and down to give the okay.

Quickly, Simpson gave special attention to two envelopes with recent post-marks. The first was from Frontier Airlines which appeared to be a frequent flier awards envelope.

The second was from High Point Landscaping Company, Littleton, Colorado. Simpson had picked out these two envelopes in less than thirty seconds. He became concerned Ivey might become alarmed and notify the Denver Police Department.

"Mr. Ivey, it's a pleasure meeting you today and I really appreciate your help. If need be, may I call on you again?"

Ivey with a slight smile, "Absolutely no problem, I can use the money!" The two men parted company and Simpson headed for Littleton, Colorado.

Chapter 11

When Simpson drove on the parking lot of High Point Landscaping, a large man was entering the front door of the office building. Suddenly, he stopped on the front porch and waited for Simpson.

"Good afternoon, I'm Lester Sloan, the owner. What may I do for you today?"

"Mr. Sloan, I'm Detective Ed Simpson and I'm seeking some information. Simpson didn't hesitate in flashing his badge and credentials. He could tell Sloan was surprised to have a detective on premise.

"Come on in, I'll help you anyway I can!"

"Mr. Sloan, we have reason to believe you are dealing with a gentlemen by the name of Andrew Scoggins and we need to locate him!"

Looking over at his secretary, Sloan asked, "Are we dealing with Andrew Scoggins?"

The secretary entered the Scoggins name and came up with an account number and mailing address. The computer print-out listed, Mr. Andrew Scoggins at 3104 Squawline, Littleton, Colorado. The telephone number, email address and other related information had been deleted. She handed the vital information to Mr. Sloan.

Sloan looking inquisitive, "Now, Detective Simpson why don't you tell me what this is all about?"

"Well, about all I can say is, Mr. Scoggins was injured and he checked out of a hospital early without authorization. That's about all I know at this time. I do appreciate your help today."

Simpson's intuition told him it was time to clear the premise. He needed to check out Squawline Drive as quickly as possible! Looking at his watch, he had two hours before his bar date with, Kathy McBride. He didn't want to miss-out on teaching her the 'in's and out's' of the oil business! As he checked the Littleton City map he found Squawline Drive to be in an upscale neighborhood and he estimated the home values between $250,000 and $400,000.

He pulled his rent car up in front of 3104 Squawline Drive and slowly walked up the sidewalk to the front porch. The home was of English Tudor design and the premises were well kept. When he approached the front door, the lawn sprinkler system was activated on the west side of the front lawn. Maybe he was about to get a break and meet Scoggins face to face!

Suddenly, he heard an elderly ladies voice from the east side of the front lawn. "Good afternoon young man, may I help you in someway?"

"Yes maam, I am looking for, Mr. Andrew Scoggins!"

The reply came swiftly, "Young man, you must have the wrong address. I live next door, and there's no, Mr. Scoggins living here.

"No sir, I've lived next door for about four years, never heard of a Scoggins!"

"I appreciate your time this afternoon, do you mind telling me who lives here?"

"Yes sir, now who are you?"

"I'm detective, Ed Simpson."

Smiling, the elderly lady said, "Let me see some I.D."

Slowly, pulling out his detective badge, he flashed it in front of her face. She immediately grabbed him by the right wrist, "My goodness, Mr. Simpson you're a long way from home! What did this Scoggins fellow do?"

"Maam, it's a long story and looks as though I'm at a dead end."

"Well, since you are a nice detective, I'll just tell you about Mr. Abbott. He's the fellow who lived here. But I didn't see him much after the terrible accident. I guess it's been several years since that happened. They were such a nice family. After his wife and children were killed in that accident, Mr. Abbott was never the same. He didn't stay home very much. He was killed somewhere overseas shortly after their funeral."

"Maam I don't mean to impose on you, maybe you could describe the Abbott family."

"Detective Simpson, I don't see how it would help you since your looking for a, Mr. Scoggins."

"Well, to be honest maam, I'm not sure who I'm trying to find at this point!"

"Tell you what young man, you come back tomorrow afternoon about 2:00 pm. and I will see if I can remember some more about those fine people."

As Simpson drove off Squawline Drive he felt uneasy about his conversation with one elderly lady living next door! The uneasy feeling would call for him to change his rent car. Only one hour remaining before he was to meet with Kathy McBride, he had to hurry.

When he arrived at the hotel he had another sensation come over him as he approached his room.

He found the door partially open, his clothes were off the rack and scattered throughout the room. The dresser drawers were upside down laying on the bed, with some of his personal items laying in front of the T.V. A feeling of frustration came over him, along with a feeling he had personally been violated. He thought quickly about calling hotel security, then he had a second thought. If he were to react in that manner he would blow his cover, so for now the crime would not be reported. So far, he had been good in making judgment calls and for now he would go it alone.

Chapter 12

It was exactly 2012 hours when Simpson walked into the hotel bar,'The Lions Den. Quickly glancing around the room he did not see, Kathy McBride. He walked up to the bar and asked, Eddie the bar keep if he might have a message. "No sir," came the reply. Since most ladies are a few minutes late on occasion he decided to relax with a double scotch and water. He seated himself at the bar where he had good vision of the entry way. After three scotch and waters he decided to move to the hotel restaurant for a good meal before retiring for the evening.

When Simpson walked into his room the phone light was blinking. He pushed the message button and realized Kathy McBride had left a message. The message related she was still in a business meeting and would contact him later. At this point all kinds of thoughts raced across Simpson's mind. First and foremost, she was thoughtful enough to let him know she could not make their meeting. Then too, she planned to contact him later which was pleasing to his ear.

It was now 2300 hours and bedtime. As he turned back the bed covers, suddenly the hotel parking lot underneath his third floor room became a busy place! Four Denver Police Squad Cars, ambulance, and fire resuscitation personnel ran toward the hotel entry way.

Simpson quickly called the hotel desk clerk, Simpson asked, "What's going on?"

The clerk responded in a quivering voice, "A woman has been killed on the fifth floor!"

The last time Simpson moved so quickly was in 'Nam when he was involved in his first fire fight! He was on the elevator before he remembered he had not tied his shoe laces. When he stepped into the fifth floor hallway, he was met head-on by Sgt. Clarence Bowie.

"Sorry mister, this floor is closed," Bowie advised.

Simpson was most respectful of Bowie's position, with a slight smile he informed him he was an officer of the law from Chicago and presented his credentials. Officer Bowie, I'm in town on business may I be of assistance?"

"No thanks, Simpson the coroner is on his way, along with our forensic unit, we have a deceased white female who apparently was murdered."

Leaning toward Bowie in a low voice, Simpson inquired, "Do you have a name as yet?"

"Yes, McBride, looks as though she was shot between the eyes as she opened her door."

Simpson's knees buckled and he turned white as he leaned back against the wall. While he regained his composure, Lt. James Harvel approached.

"I understand your are Detective Simpson from Chicago. Seems to me you're a long way from home. What brings you to the Denver area?"

"I'm doing special work for International Oil & Gas. Are you familiar with them?"

"Nope!" Do you know this young lady, Ms. McBride, the deceased?"

"No. However, I did meet her at the restaurant down the street and we had breakfast together. I was suppose to meet her this evening but she didn't show."

Lt. James Harvel leaned forward toward Simpson, placing his left hand on the wall so he could draw closer, he said "Yankee, you move pretty damn fast don't you? This McBride woman was real pretty, but someone messed up her face with a 9mm! I'll guess you wouldn't have a clue about that, would you?"

"If you mean about somebody killing her, no! I have to admit she was good-looking and what I thought was a 'keeper'," replied Simpson.

"Well, just goes to show you how wrong you can be, you are lucky to be alive! I'll need to visit with you after the coroner and our forensic team complete their findings. What's your room number?"

"Room 320."

Harvel frowning, "Simpson, don't leave town. I want to meet with you first thing come daylight."

Simpson felt he had somewhat been ruffed up by Lt. Harvel as he stepped into the elevator. With Harvel's attitude and his friend, Kathy McBride murdered he felt all alone in a big city without friends; maybe another scotch and water would help. Without hesitation he headed for The Lions Den. He had a lot on his mind so he would stay and help close the place down.

It was no use, Simpson could not sleep, too many thoughts and questions were constantly swirling in his mind. Who was McBride? Which side was she on? Why did Lt. Harvel want to see him at the break of dawn. Why did Harvel make the statement, 'You are lucky to be alive'?

At 0530 Simpson's phone rang. Lt. Harvel instructed him to meet him at the Alpine Restaurant in thirty-minutes.

Simpson had finished his first cup of coffee when Lt. Harvel arrived. The greetings were cordial for an early morning meeting, which seemed to be filled with an air of suspense and uncertainty.

"Have you ordered?" asked Harvel.

"Not yet. I'm still trying to wake up. You guys here in Denver sure come to work early! What's this meeting about? I guess you're picking up the tab on this one, since you invited me at this most inconvenient time, right?"

"Yeah, I guess you are worth a meal, if you'll be honest with me, Harvel answered.

"No doubt about it, honesty is the best policy. What do you want to know?"

"You told me earlier you are doing some work for International Oil & Gas. I have reason to believe you lied to me!"

"Well, Harvel you told me you knew nothing about International, I too, believe you lied to me. The way I see it, I guess the playing field is level, would you agree?"

"Yankee, I guess you've got me there. Smiling, Let's work together and see if we can clear up this mess. Since you didn't let my department know you were in town, I sense you are working on something big. I really believe it will be beneficial to both our departments to join hands on this one."

"Agreed, I've got to check in with my Captain Turner to get approval.

"The captain asked before I came out if I had notified you guys. At that point I felt it best to go it alone, since I didn't have enough information. Before I call, Captain Turner in Chicago do you have anything you can share with me at this time?"

"Since you have an interest in International Oil & Gas' operation, we're led to believe the company is involved in clandestine activity." Harvel answered.

"You mentioned last evening that I was lucky to be alive! What did you mean by that remark?"

"Kathy McBride is from the Chicago area and she did not work for Paramount Modeling Agency in New York. Somehow, she knew you were trying to identify the, Wolf and so was she. Our information shows she had some affiliation with the Corzion drug cartel out of South America, probably Columbia!

"We've been working with the FBI for about six months on this and they are our main source, plus we do have some informants in this immediate area. Our respective, Wolf has been a busy boy over the last three days. I pulled this information from our FBI internet connection. Take a look, as a matter of fact you may share this information with, Chief Turner."

Smiling, Harvel handed Simpson a brown envelop marked, 'Secret'. It contained three recent FBI reports covering bombings in Miami, San Francisco, and New Orleans. Each report reflected the, Wolf was responsible. He inflicted death to gang members who were dealing in narcotics, prostitution and human trafficking. One report from the FBI, San Francisco office listed thirty-six teenagers, (thirty girls and six boys) from Calcutta had been freed.

"Harvel, can your department identify the, Wolf?"

"No! I can tell you one better, neither can the FBI, or the CIA identify him. This man is truly a wolf. Some individuals might refer to him as a vigilante, but we really believe it goes far beyond that scenario. Somewhere down the line he apparently had some kind of connection with USMC.; however the FBI and CIA cannot make the connection. No doubt about it, this is a strange case.

Now, enlighten me about what you have accomplished here in Denver, and share with me the knowledge you gleaned in Chicago."

"It's apparent you folks here in Denver have been blessed with data out of FBI office in Chicago.

I'll not cover that particular data now. As far as what I've learned here in Denver it is very limited other than what you have furnished. I'm still trying to figure out International Oil and Gas Corporation. For example, is Andrew Scoggins and Ann Duval for real? It seems the building superintendent at the Page building has seen these individuals."

"Oh yes, I wanted to talk to you about your dealings with our, Mr. Ivey. May I suggest you quit paying him a $100 for information. The going rate is $25.00, replied

Harvel. Simpson commented, "Don't tell me he's on your department's payroll."

Laughing, Harvel answered. "Only as needed. I think he's on everybody's payroll."

The two men realized they could not properly identify Andrew Scoggins or Ann Duval.

As the two men parted company, Simpson was still in a quandary as to who murdered the pretty Kathy McBride.

Chapter 13

The Attorney General's office received an email message which was short and read. The Wolf is on the prowl! Wire monies Western Union, St. Louis, Missouri! It didn't take long for the Attorney General to comply with a $10,000 advance and a note of reply which read, "Continue your hunt, good luck."

Abbott, the Wolf, phoned Helen Schroeder, aka, Ann Duval to furnish additional information regarding the scheduled hunt in the St. Louis area. As Helen answered her phone she heard a faint howl. She decided to play the game.

"Hello, this is the den mother!"

Abbott responded, "That's one of the reasons I enjoy doing business with you. It doesn't take long for you to adjust to any situation. At this point, I won't mention the other reasons."

"The reason you won't mention the other reasons is why I like you!"

"Good enough reason, one of the reasons I called is I need an update on Snider, have you heard from him?"

"Yes, I met him in Denver, Colorado. Snider said you had a Detective Simpson from Chicago on your tail; likewise, you had a good looking blonde named, McBride trying to terminate you. McBride was with the Corzion Cartel, so I eliminated her!"

"Helen, you could wait until I have a chance to become better acquainted with the ladies before terminating them."

"I don't think so, I'm trying to keep you alive. To be honest, I don't know why!"

"Dearest Helen, maybe it's best left unsaid. In our line of work longevity is in short supply. Speaking of supply, I'm running short on C-4 compound and ammunition. Please forward a package via Central Bus Lines to St. Louis, Missouri. When you talk to Snider tell him I'm moving to Seattle,Washington after this assignment and I would like for the two of you to join me. When we meet I'll bring you folks up to date. Got to go, check the St. Louis Chronicle for an update in Sunday's paper."

Again, without further conversation the phone line went open. The Wolf left the line without saying goodbye.

Helen immediately called Dave Snider, informant extraordinaire.

Dave answered his cell phone out of breath. "Hello, I'm here."

Helen pressed the phone close to her left ear. "Snider, you sound pooped, what's up?"

"Hi Helen, I've been working out and I think I have pulled a back muscle. Don't let folks kid you about this growing old being fun!. What have you got?"

"I just heard from the Wolf, he wants us to meet him in Seattle, Washington. He left the phone in a hurry but he'll be calling back soon. What's going on?"

"It's a big deal. I've got my ear to the ground on this one. I can't talk to you on the phone about the deal, I'll share the information when we meet. Oh, by the way you did a good job on McBride. From what I was told, she definitely was going to 'pop', Simpson after he led her to the Wolf!"

"Thanks for the compliment. I was just trying to keep our man alive," answered Helen.

As the two prepared to hang up the phone, Helen suddenly thought about how much Dave Snider meant to Steve Hightower and her during their FBI days. To be able to hold a friendship over several years in their line of work was remarkable. Just before hanging up the phone, Helen remarked, "Thanks, Snider for being my friend. I'll meet you in the lobby of the Melrose Hotel, in Seattle, Friday afternoon at 1630 hours. I'll be visiting with the Wolf this Sunday evening and I'll do my best to keep you informed."

"I'll see you Friday week at the Melrose," Snider replied.

The next few days seemed rather long and without major incidents. During this period Helen prepared C-4 compound, while giving particular attention to the packaging. Just to be on the safe side she would prepare additional packaging for the fuses and the 40 mm ammunition.

With luck in shipping via bus line the Wolf would have his requested supplies by Thursday evening. In today's world her business seemed to be changing daily. Nowadays, with new technology you best have a good working plan, and an alternate plan which had been time tested.

To ship the Wolf his supplies, Helen would again take on the roll of Ann Duvall, CIA agent.

Posing as a CIA agent came natural for Helen, aka, Ann Duval. She had played the part so many times it was becoming her alter ego. Dressed in a black business suit, white blouse, black high heels, with her black raincoat draped over her left arm she entered the Central Bus Line terminal. Quickly reconnoitering the interior of the station she noticed two arm policemen stationed at each of the exit doors for boarding the buses. She had wrapped her eight pound package carefully and it was marked properly to pass security. En route to the shipping counter she had been offered assistance by two marines and one navy man. She had shown courtesy in rejecting their offers. By doing so, she had caught the attention of one of the security guards.

As he approached he was smiling and had every intention of getting better acquainted with this good-looking lady.

"Maam, I notice several have offered their assistance, I do hope you will not refuse me."

"Officer, I'm delighted you noticed but my package is not heavy and I can manage."

"Well, you do appear to be a lady who can handle most situations but I insist!"

Ann handed him the package marked, for delivery to 'Agent Andrew Scoggins, CIA,' ST. Louis, Missouri. Recognizing the officer had a look of dismay, Ann immediately presented her credentials.

"Hold fast maam, I'm afraid I'll have to clear you with Central Bus Line Security's office."

Ann looked at the officer's name badge, "Officer Hadley that's fine; however we do have a problem here. This package must be delivered to the CIA Agent.

"You'll notice the form attached has Chicago's CIA Division authorization and must reach it's destination on time."

Smiling, Officer Hadley said, "Tell you what, pretty lady if you will have a drink with me I'll personally place the package aboard. Is that a fair deal?"

In Ann Duval's mind set, she had just hit a home run out of the park. "Is that all you want, Officer Hadley?"

"Not really but it's a starter. Let me check off duty and we'll go over to Sammy's bar across the street, okay?"

"Fine with me," Ann replied. For the next seven minutes she watched Hadley as he talked to the baggage clerk and check the package. In the process both Hadley and the clerk had a few chuckles. She could only surmise Hadley had let the clerk know he had a 'hot one' setting on ready. She watched Hadley load the package on a bus bound for St. Louis, Missouri. Let the fun time begin!

Sammy's bar was a cozy little place. A good bar with six tables and eight booths. It was extra clean and didn't have a smoky odor. Sammy greeted Hadley as though they were long lost brothers and Hadley introduced Ann as his best friend of long standing.

Sammy was a charmer. "Little lady, what will be your pleasure this evening?"

"I'll have a double Chivas Regal and water," Ann replied.

Smiling, Hadley said, "The lady has exceptionally good taste . . . make mine the same." Hadley's mood became more amorous as he kissed Ann's right hand.

After a lot of get acquainted conversation and four rounds of scotch whiskey, Hadley made his move. When

Ann returned from the ladies room and was seated in the booth, Hadley reached his left hand underneath the table and placed it between Ann's legs. Suddenly, Ann moved to the outside of the seat.

Ann with a firm look, "Hadley, you seem like a likeable guy and I sure don't care to disappoint you but the eager beaver stuff is not my modus operandi. It's just not my style."

"Look lady, I've done you a big favor tonight and I expect reciprocation. You know you want me and you're playing games. You knew the game was on when we left the bus terminal."

"Well, I have to admit I could tell you were horny, but I had a job to do. I'm sorry I have miss-led you but I must go."

Angrily, Hadley said, "You're not going anywhere until you 'put-out'! He reached over and grabbed Ann's hair and pulled her down in the seat. Moving around the table top he now had her pinned to the seat, with Ann's left arm pulled behind her left shoulder and he was applying pressure. With his left hand he unbuttoned the top four buttons of her blouse and began massaging her left breast in hopes she would give it. If not, he had made up his mind he would rape her in the booth. With it being a late hour and Sammy in the kitchen to close up shop, he felt he was in total control. Ann begin to breathe hard as though his tactics were working. Hadley became more aroused and let up the pressure. Slowly Ann twisted her body so he was on top.

The maneuver allowed her to reach her waist band for a very small canister of mace. Hadley was an easy target since he was now directly on top of her. Ann let loose a long blast of mace directly into his face. He let out a loud scream and literally rolled into the floor and grasped tables and chairs to steady himself as he was trying to reach the men's restroom to wash his eyes.

Ann called out to Sammy, "Sammy, Hadley needs help he's had an accident!"

Alarmed, Sammy asked, "What the hell happened to my friend?"

"He will be okay in a short while, we had a little disagreement over sex! Here's a $100 to cover the bar bill. The big man may want to visit a clinic to have his eyes flushed. I had to hit him with a good shot of mace to keep him from doing something he would always regret. You may feel free to call Chicago's finest, but I seriously doubt he would want you to do that. I'm out of here!"

Ann stepped out the front door of Sammy's where a taxi was on station. She thought to herself, 'What a night to remember.' Of course, the real important part to remember was, the Wolf would have his supplies to finish his assignment in St. Louis, Missouri.

Chapter 14

St. Louis, Missouri.

Jack Abbott, the Wolf had received his package from Ann Duval. At precisely 2318 hours, he opened the front door to Mac McIlroy's Pub, situated in downtown St. Louis. As he made his entry he could not help but notice the leaded glass doors and the polished brass door handles. In an odd way he somewhat felt guilty for entering a pristine facility because within a few minutes it would not look the same due to a lot of collateral damage.

He took off his back-pack and placed it in the coat room over the half-doors which served as a check-out counter. Few patrons even noticed he entered with a back-pack which contained enough explosives to start a small war. The inventory included four smoke grenades, six small packages of C-4 compound with fuses time set, one hundred rounds for his 9mm Glock, a back-up stiletto switchblade knife, plus duct tape and other assorted items. He placed a silver wolf signet on the coat check-out counter. When he turned to enter the bar area, he felt a large hand on his right shoulder. Looking up he was facing a huge man with a friendly smile, a club bouncer.

"Good evening, Sir. Welcome to Mac's place," the huge man said.

"It's good to be here. I'm looking for a little excitement," the Wolf replied.

"I couldn't help but notice you stowed a back-pack in the coat room."

"Yep, kinda hard to dance to the lively music with a back-pack strapped to my shoulders."

Now frowning, the big man said, "Let's take a look inside the pack."

There was no reply as the bouncer leaned over the half doors to reach the pack. He slowly pulled out the stiletto switchblade knife and inserted the six-inch blade just above the man's first vertebrae causing instant death. The big man let out a muffled sound and slumped across the half doors. He quickly pushed him inside the coat room to conceal his body, grabbing his back-pack, it was time to go to work. He had done his home work as he knew every nook and cranny of the facility. Most importantly he knew the contents of the establishment, the number of working personnel, the number of prostitutes working the bar and dance floor areas.

He had given special attention to the forty teenage Mexican females being held hostage in the basement.

As the 'Outrigger Band' was really cranking out lively tunes, the drunks and prostitutes were trying to keep up with the beat. It gave the Wolf opportunity to move in and out of the crowd to place the C-4 compound charges in strategic locations. He mixed and mingled with the crowd. Within thirty minutes the place would be a hell hole. He planted a C-4 charges underneath the bar, and over the entry into the men's room.

So far so good, however he had not spotted Mac McIlroy and it was important to take him out during this operation. From the men's room he moved directly down stairs to the basement area.

As he turned left at the bottom of the stairs he came face to face with Mac's body guard. A blond headed man standing well over six foot, three inches and well built.

The guard was the first to speak, "You must be lost, the dancing is upstairs."

The Wolf did not reply, he quicken his pace toward the guard, simultaneously pulling his Glock 9mm while firing one round hitting the guard between the eyes. He thought, why would a body guard be in the basement . . . just maybe, Mac was being a bad boy and mis-treating the Mexican girls held captive; his assessment was correct!

Now to locate the girls. Again, he quickened his pace as he moved down the hallway, stopping briefly at each door trying to hear a sound. Suddenly, in the room across the hall, he heard a whimper from a young girl and Mac's voice assuring the young female she would enjoy having him take her. Without warning, he kicked the door open and came face to face with Mac. It was no contest, as he thrust his right hand into Mac's throat crushing his larynx, he then led with his left forearm smashing Mac's nose, while jamming the nose bone up and into his brain. Within four seconds McIroy was history. Glancing at his watch, he had only eighteen minutes to lead the girls to safety, notify authorities and clear the bar and dance hall upstairs of all personnel. At this juncture the party goer's had no clue they were in harms way!

Looking at the captives he held his hands high in the air, "Signa muy cerca", they understood they were to follow close behind. He immediately opened the two coal-bin doors which led to the alley, and they walked out of the coal-bin into the alleyway. Now they were safe. He instructed them to wait for the policia!

He immediately called a 911 operator on his cell phone, with explicit instructions to notify the Police and Mercy Hospital, requesting nurses, ambulance services, Fire Department and the Welfare Division to take care of the forty young ladies now in his custody. As usual the 911 operator wanted more information.

"Sir, I need more information. What's your name?"

The response was quick and sharp, "Wolf!"

"Where are you located?"

"The alley behind Mac McIlroy's Pub," he responded.

"Do you have anyone injured?"

"Yes operator, I have killed three people and I'm about to blow-up the Pub."

Now the operator's voice reflected anxiety, "Sir, please stay on the line I have help coming!"

"Operator, I appreciate your position; however I can't stay in contact. There's almost two hundred people inside this building and I've got to get them out." The operator's phone line went open.

He had the young Mexican girls follow him down the alley to the east corner of the building, while assuring them he would be back to help them see a de cabecera. The comment seemed to calm the group as they understood they would have the opportunity to see a doctor.

Turning to urgent business at hand he headed upstairs to the dance floor. It was imperative he reach the microphone. Moving rapidly to the dance stand he seized the mike from the band director.

"Sir, pardon me. We have an emergency situation here." The band director stepped back.

"Ladies and gentlemen, it is necessary you leave this building immediately! I want you to move in an orderly way to the front of the building. When you reach the street move to the left past the parking lot."

A middle aged man who had been drinking way beyond his capacity said, "Who in the hell are you, the Fire Marshall?"

"No, I'm a bomber," the Wolf replied. He took a smoke grenade from his pack and pulled the pin, while turning to his right he threw it behind the bar. Within six seconds smoke begin to fill the room. A slight smile came across his face, as he watched the middle aged man, who was somewhat inebriated become sober in a big time hurry!

The patrons begin to move out into the street as sirens blared with official help on the way. The C-4 charges were shaped to do minimum damage to the inside of the building and the Fire Department would be able to control the fire without damage to the adjacent buildings. After all was said and done, the world would be a much better place without McIlroy and his thugs who prayed on the young. Another assignment completed the Wolf would move on to Seattle,Washington, via Chicago.

The Chicago visit was vital since he needed additional combat supplies, and needed to glean additional information from Helen. The Wolf had received word from a merchant marine informant, that the ship Lenora had left the port of Lisbon, Portugal ten days earlier. She set sail with two prominent drug lords aboard. The initial information received indicated they were to be joined by at least two other drug lords for a strategic planning session to be held in Seattle. Since the Lenora was a major target, the Wolf wanted to participate in the meeting!

Chapter 15

Denver, Colorado . . . . 0618 Hours.

The phone in Detective Ed Simpson's room begin ringing loudly, arousing him from a sound sleep. With his eyes shut he slowly reached for the phone instrument and knocked it off the table next to his bed. His first thought was 'who would be calling him before the chickens left their roost'. Slowly he gathered his senses and picked up the phone receiver.

"Yeah, what's up?"

"You should be, you lazy bastard! I understand from Marty Stewart you tried to call me. I guess you have found this Scoggins fellow. Is that right?"

"No sir. I was calling to tell you I have made contact with the Denver Police Department, or maybe I should say, they've made contact with me."

"Simpson, I've been contacted by the FBI office here in Chicago. I guess, Detective Harvel has informed them you arc involved in this case. By the way, who in the hell is Kathy McBride? This report indicates she got herself killed messing around with you!"

"No sir, let me explain."

"Simpson, you can explain it when I review your expense report. You catch the next flight to Chicago, we've got a lot of work to do."

"Chief, allow me the opportunity to re-check a lead I have in Littleton, Colorado. I think I got close to this Scoggins fellow. It will take me about four to six hours more work. Will that meet with your approval?"

"Yeah, go ahead. I don't know why I allow you to 'put me together' on these wild goose chases. Don't get yourself 'whacked'. I want to hear more about this Kathy McBride, I know she'll be listed somewhere on your expense statement! I'll see you promptly at 0830 hours day after tomorrow. Don't be late!"

A quick breakfast at the Alpine Restaurant brought back fond memories of Kathy McBride, Simpson could still see that flirtatious smile, then soberly he remembered, Lt Harvel telling him he was lucky to be alive. At least she had made the trip to Denver pleasant up until her demise.

When he drove up in front of High Point Landscaping company he noticed a crew of men loading several shrubs and tools on a flatbed truck, no Lester Sloan the owner. A man standing near the truck was issuing orders as Simpson approached.

"Good morning, looks as though you fellows are getting an early start," remarked Simpson."

Quickly, Simpson flashed his credentials. After a short conversation Simpson asked about their work in Littleton. The foreman was familiar with the area and had briefly visited with a Mrs. Abbott at the 3104 Squawline address. He did not know anyone by the name of Scoggins; however on one occasion he had met one of Mr. Abbott's golfing buddies who lived at 3119 Squawline Drive. Hurriedly, Simpson thanked the work crew and headed for Squawline Drive. Sure enough as he slowly drove by the 3104 address there was the elderly lady working her flower bed next door. Hopefully, it would not be necessary to visit with her again.

As he drove up in front of the 3119 address a middle aged lady was placing outgoing mail in her mail box.

"Good morning, Maam. May I have a moment of your time?"

"Yes sir, I'm Nancy Wilson how may I help you?"

As Simpson presented his credentials he said,"I'm trying to contact the folks who live at the 3104 address. Would you happen to know them?"

"Oh yes, we knew them. My husband played golf with, Jack Abbott frequently, Connie Abbott and I were good friends. That is such a tragic story. Why are you inquiring about the Abbott's at this time? Does it have anything to do with their estate?"

"No maam, I thought Andrew Scoggins lived at that address. Maybe I have the two men mixed up. Would you describe, Jack Abbott to me and what happened to him and his family?"

"Well, Jack was about your size, I would say about six foot, one hundred and ninety pounds, blond hair and fair complexion. My dear friend, Connie was five foot eight inches and extremely well built. The two children, Michael, seven and Evelyn his sister was five.

Connie and the children were killed in a car accident near Estes Park. Jack was never the same after that. He was a tough man, war hero and all but was not able to cope with losing his family! Some mutual friends told my husband, Jack just gave up after his family was killed. We understand he was working overseas and killed in a drilling rig accident.

"What type of work did Jack Abbott perform?"

"Oh, I believe he worked as a Petroleum Engineer for International Oil & Gas. I do remember he traveled the world over. Connie was always complaining about him being gone so much."

"I would like to meet your husband. Would that be possible?"

"I'm sorry, I lost Jerry to Leukemia a little over a year ago."

"Mrs. Wilson, I'm so sorry to hear of your loss."

"That's okay, you had no way of knowing. I hope I have helped you in someway."

"You have, and I am most grateful. One other question, you mentioned the Estate. Do you know who looks after the Estate?"

"Yes, Jerry told me International Oil & Gas was in charge of the Estate." Simpson wished, Nancy Wilson the best, and went to the hotel to check out. He needed to call Harvel.

"Lt. Harvel, good morning. I'm returning your call. What's up?"

"Just thought I'd check to see if you were still alive. Have you met another good-looking blonde as you travel the Denver area?"

"Nope! I'm fresh out of blondes. I'm glad you called. I'm checking out of the hotel as we speak. Captain Turner has ordered me back to Chicago. I want to thank you for your support while I've been in town. If and when you come to Chicago I'll reciprocate."

"Sounds like a deal to me. I'll phone you in a few days. Have a safe trip." Lt. Harvel hung up the phone. When Ed Simpson reached Denver International Airport he made a quick phone call to Chicago Police Headquarters and instructed Marty to check with Colorado's Secretary of State's office to locate the principals of International Oil and Gas. In addition, he asked she check with Littleton, Colorado's Land Appraisal District office to determine who owned the property located at 3104 Squawline Drive. He also instructed her to send an email to USMC, Attention:

Intelligence Division to confirm as to whether or not, Jack Abbott or Andrew Scoggins served in Iraq. He explained this was truly a blind lead and he would explain fully when he returned to his office.

Chapter 16

It was raining again when, Jack Abbott's taxi pulled up in front of Helen Schroeder' s apartment. Even though it was late he felt he would be welcome. After all, the small lamp was still on in the living room. Even though Helen did not know the exact hour of his arrival, he had told her he would be coming to Chicago before the 'deal' went down in Seattle, Washington. She certainly would be a welcome sight and she would be able to provide him safe shelter for a couple of days. He gently knocked four times on the front door . . . . Helen did not respond. Putting his ear to the door, he could here music playing. He immediately recognized the tune, 'The Sweetest Thing

I've Ever Known Is Loving You.' Suddenly, he thought she might have a guest!

Abbott moved swiftly to the back of the house. As he peered through the kitchen window, he viewed a dark haired man seated directly across the dining table from Helen. Since it was pouring down rain, his sounds were muffled as he moved quickly back to the front porch and picked up his back pack. It was time to find a motel room for the night! He walked three blocks east to Jake's bar and grill and called a taxi. An hour later he was comfortable in Room #130 at the Roadside Inn. In the quiet of the motel room he could not help but wonder who the dark haired man might be. He decided he would ask Helen come morning. For now he was in bad need of some 'shut-eye'.

It was 0830 hours when he opened his eyes and viewed the bright sun shining against the curtains in his room. He had not intended to sleep so long but apparently he needed the rest.

First things first, he needed to talk with Helen Schroeder to make sure they were in agreement regarding the trip to Seattle. Due to his equipment and all the 'hardware supplies' needed, it would be necessary for

Helen to drive because they would never clear security at Chicago's Midway airport.

When Abbott's taxi pulled up in front of Helen's apartment, she was in the front yard picking up her newspaper. A big smile came across her face when Abbott came into view.

"Good morning," she yelled.

Smiling, Abbott said, "Good morning to you pretty lady."

"Come inside and I'll treat you to a good breakfast."

"That's the best offer I've had today," replied Abbott.

While Helen was making breakfast, Abbott decided to shave and freshen up a bit.

Within fifteen minutes Helen shouted, "Come and get it. The coffee is hot and I hope you are hungry."

As Abbott walked into the kitchen area he started to ask about the dark haired man who was seated in his chair last evening. But he held his tongue, because he knew it was none of his business. Helen would tell him if she felt it was important in their personal relationship. He decided to keep the conversation on the business level . . . Seattle, Washington!

Helen opened the conversation. "I checked **The Chronicle** paper out of St. Louis and the paper gave you a good review. It's a shame the only identity they could give you was the Wolf, because of the signet you left behind. I'm always amazed as to how thorough they can be while looking through debris, C-4 charge desolation, smoke grenades and you name it, yet they still can come up with your small wolf signet as evidence."

"Listen, I hate to change the subject. I must move rapidly since I have to reconnoiter the Seattle area. Did you set up a meeting with Snider?"

"I did. I'm sending him a new ID packet, he'll be known as Doug Taylor and we're to meet at the Melrose Hotel in Shoreline,Washington Friday evening. I'll carry the ID of Marie Higgins, CIA Agent. We'll be about ten minutes from the Brown Hotel. Here's your ID packet, Jack Harris**,** Independent Oil Operator."

"Will this give you adequate time to make the long drive?"

"Yes, I already have your supplies and my luggage packed. I'm ready to drive you to the Midway Airport when you are ready. I would appreciate you filling me in on some details, like what the hell's going on? I work better when I know the metes and bounds!"

"Helen, I'm sorry that's an oversight on my part. There's been so much happening in putting this deal together. We have a big drug cartel meeting coming down in Seattle. There will be at least four cartels represented by leaders and co-leaders of each cartel, plus bodyguards galore. I have already confirmed the Corizon group have checked into the Brown Hotel and are preparing for this meeting. I don't want to miss this one!"

When Abbott boarded Northwest flight #286, he gave particular attention to those individuals who might be air marshals, police officers or unsavory characters. His training had taught him to be alert, inquisitive, dubious, and not to trust anybody. Then verify! He was seated in row eighteen, aisle seat, on the left side which gave him a good view of the flight attendants as they preformed their duties If all went as planned, he would arrive in Seattle by 1942 hours. and check into the hotel as Jack Harris, Independent Oil Operator.

On the other hand Helen Schroeder aka., Marie Higgins, CIA Agent, was slowly making progress as she drove from Chicago westward to Minneapolis, MN. She made sure her driving habits were in line because she could not afford to be stopped by any law enforcement officer. As she pulled into the Hilltop Motel parking lot, she noticed a late model black Ford sedan pulled slowly in behind her. As she viewed the vehicle through her rear view mirror she saw one of two men light a cigarette. She did not need a problem at this point because of her cargo. If she had a confrontation it needed to occur off motel premises! Hurriedly she drove up to the motel office and checked in. She desperately wanted to alarm the motel clerk about the two men but she decided silence would be the best policy. The two men approached her car. They appeared to be Hispanic, early thirties, well built and a little on the grungy side. As they drew close to her car, she could smell alcohol. Now she was facing two drunks who apparently wanted a woman! When she stepped out of her vehicle, she slipped out one of her credit cards from her purse and cupped it in the palm of her right hand, leaving her bag on the front seat. She locked her car.

"Senorita, you come with us we'll show you good time."

"Where will you take me?"

"Oh, Senorita, we go to the river and have good time. Bring you back when you have enough!"

"Do you promise to bring me back after I give you mucho?"

"Si, Senorita we have mucho to give you!"

Now she was in somewhat of a dilemma. First she had to protect herself at all cost and without police intervention. Based on her training, she was confident she could handle the two drunks in a public place; however, based on her mission and cargo it would be a necessity to choose a very private setting. She made a quick judgment call. Leave the public parking lot.

She gripped the credit card tightly!

"How long will you keep me?"

"Until you satisfied!"

"What are your names?"

"I'm Carlos, his name is Freddie, he is timido. I take you first you have big nalgas!"

"Carlos, you say Freddie is timid and you like big bottoms, huh?"

"Si, you speak Spanish?"

"Some, let's go!" Freddie quickly took the drivers spot. Carlos put his arm around Marie's waist and pulled her toward the back seat of the car, trying to kiss her as they entered the car.

As they crossed the Buffalo River bridge, Freddie did a sharp right turn and drove under the bridge. Carlos was having difficulty unbuttoning Marie's blouse. As he placed his head on her breast, she grabbed him by his hair with her left hand, while pulling him back she pulled the sharp credit card across his face! Carlos let out a loud scream as the blood begin to flow from his forehead, nose and left cheek. Freddie was in the process of stopping the car. Suddenly, he looked toward the rear seat as Carlos was fighting to get out of the car. Marie put her left arm around Freddie's forehead and raked the credit card across his neck hitting the jugular vein causing Freddie to literally roll out of the car. Both would be attackers were now naturalized and suffering from blood loss and severe pain.

Marie proceeded to take charge of the car and quickly drove back up on Eastern Avenue and headed back toward the motel. She decided to abandon Freddie's vehicle on a side street at Faulkner Avenue, three blocks from the motel. Her blouse and the front of her skirt were covered in blood ; it was essential she clean up and check out of the Hilltop Motel. At this point she had no way of knowing how Carlos and Freddie would react to their awkward situation. Her intuition told her it would be best to continue to drive westward. Within a short while she would stop at the nearest Truck Stop on Highway 94 and catch a couple hours sleep.

Chapter 17

Marty escorted Ed Simpson into Captain Turner's office at 0912 hours. "Ed, since the Captain is running a little late this morning, may I bring you a cup of coffee while you are waiting?"

"You're a sweetheart. Say, have you received a report back from the Secretary of State's office in Colorado regarding the ownership of International Oil & Gas?" Smiling, Marty said, "Are you for real? Don't you ever think about anything other than business?"

"Yep, sure do. Sometimes I think about monkey business or just fooling around! How about you?"

"You fool! The replies from the Secretary of State's office and the Denver Appraisal District are on your desk. We haven't heard a word from the USMC. And yes, sometimes I think about fooling around."

"Marty, good job. I'd best review those replies before I visit with Captain Turner. I'll be back in a jiffy."

Hurriedly, Simpson made it to his office. He only hoped and prayed he would have time to review the items before Captain Turner arrived. If he appeared to be late, it would not help his cause as far as the Captain was concerned. It was time to prepare himself by obtaining a mind set which would allow him to be pleasing and optimistic in his Captain's view.

As he reviewed the Secretary of State's report, it reflected International Oil & Gas principals were Mr. Andrew Scoggins, President, CEO and Ann Duvall, Secretary-Treasurer. The state filings were up to date and in order with no other officers of the corporation listed.

The other report from the Denver Appraisal reflected the properties located at 3104 Squawline Drive, were owned by Mr. Andrew Scoggins with no other party listed. The school, county and state taxes had been paid and there were no liens against the properties. Simpson remembered the hot cup of coffee Marty had delivered in the Captain's office.

He quickly gathered up his replies and phone messages which had been left in his absence then headed back to the Captain's office. Captain Turner was now seated behind his desk with his blasted cigar going full bore. Simpson put on a big smile as he entered the office.

"Oh, you finally decided to show up for work." Captain Turner barked!

"Yes sir, I just couldn't bare being away from you any longer. By the way, you're drinking my coffee."

"I don't think so."

"Yes sir, I was in here earlier and Marty brought me the cup!"

"Well, excuse the hell out of me. Do you think she might show a little courtesy to the chief and bring him a cup?"

"Chief, I'm not sure. Please allow me to get you a fresh cup. I'll be right back."

When Simpson reached the hallway, there stood Marty with two fresh cups of coffee.

"Smiling, Simpson asked, "When would you consider 'fooling around'?"

"When you have a lot of money", came the sharp and pointed answer. Marty made a hasty exit from the room.

Simpson gave a compete summary on his work and stay while in the Denver area, including the response from the Secretary of State's office and the Denver Appraisal District. After all was said and done, it was not enough information to assist in finding Scoggins and Duvall. The best anyone could hope for would be a 'stakeout' at International's offices and Lt. Harvel in the Denver Police Department would have to be able to staff such an effort.

For now, Captain Turner wanted Simpson to turn in all his expenses and give him more details about Kathy McBride. His reason for asking was supposedly for the Mayor's benefit, since the Mayor would be very inquisitive about her death, etc. Simpson knew he was being 'put together' as the Captain wanted to know more about his personal relationship with McBride. Simpson satisfied the Captain's itch by making up a little white lie love scene between he and Kathy. He left the Captain smiling!

When Simpson returned to his office, Irene, the switchboard operator, was calling him on the intercom.

"Simpson, I'm forwarding you a call from Chris Salazar, he's with the FBI office here in Chicago. When you review your telephone calls, you will notice he has called you several times while you were out of town. Call must be important."

"Simpson here. How may I assist you?"

"Simpson, this is FBI Agent Chris Salazar in the Chicago office. You will probably note I have left several messages for you to return my call. Have you received them?"

"Yes, I have. I just returned to Chicago last evening and it's my first day back in the office and this place is a mess. I hope I can find all four corners of my desk before the day is over. What may I do for you?"

"It may be what I can do for you," replied Salazar.

"Why don't you give me a hint as to what you're talking about."

"I'm talking about Andrew Scoggins. I understand you have been in contact with Lt. Harvel in Denver and you two have decided to work together. I'm confident Captain Turner has enlightened you that the FBI and CIA are working on the 'Wolf' case, right?"

"Yes, but he has not had time to fill me in on all the details."

"I'm sure he will later on. In the meanwhile, we need to meet. I work Counter Intelligence and I'm beginning to fit some pieces together. Let's meet at the 'Perch Bar and Grill' at 1900 hours. I know the manager and we can have a private room."

"Sounds good to me. See you at 1900 hours"

After going through all the back log of correspondence and phone messages Simpson headed for the Captain's office.

"Chief, I still have a little of the T & E money left over from the Denver trip. What about lunch today? It's on me."

"Simpson, I told you awhile back. I never turn down a free meal. You can tell me about Kathy McBride again, you may have forgotten to tell me the whole story!"

Simpson returning to his office began to plow through the back log of info before him. He recounted the phone messages from Salazar. In total, Salazar had tried to reach him five times and apparently made a personal call on Chief Turner. It was obvious this man considered their meeting urgent and needed additional information.

Hopefully, the Chief would give some clarity to the issue at lunch time. Marty stuck her head in his office and inquired as to whether or not he had caught up.

"Marty, come in here for just a minute. Were you on duty when this fellow, Chris Salazar, dropped by to visit the Chief?"

"Yes I was. This guy is a handsome dude! Well, he is Hispanic, about six foot three, slender, with coal black hair and well groomed. I didn't see a wedding ring on his left hand."

"With the well rounded report I would say you would make a good informant. I do appreciate your attention to detail," Simpson responded.

"Is that all, my Lord?"

"Get out of my office before you get into a lot of trouble." Marty turned rapidly and gave a flirtatious smile as she left the room.

The lunch period was utilized by Chief Turner and Simpson sharing not only facts concerning their case but also a lot of supposition delivered by both parties. In truth, Andrew Scoggins and Ann Duvall were still as big a mystery as they were in the beginning. But a new name had been added to the mix as the result of Simpson's trip to Denver. Now they had the man named, Jack Abbott, who once lived at the same address as Scoggins. Are they one in the same? If only the USMC Intelligence Unit would respond to Chicago Police's inquiry, it might help tie the two individuals together. At this point the USMC had not helped whatsoever!

The Abbott thing was absolutely a 'long-shot' and had no merit for full consideration at this point.

One big question seemed to be developing. Was the Federal Government involved in all this? If so, somebody had gone to a lot of trouble to cover up trails and facts. Why would the FBI be coming to Chicago's Police Department to gather data? Have the FBI, CIA been bypassed for some reason? Just how does this fellow,'Wolf', fit into the overall scheme of things. Is he actually sanctioned by the Feds to carry-out these murderous deeds? The two men enjoyed lunch time together; however, nothing was resolved concerning Andrew Scoggins and Ann Duvall.

The day had past fast for Ed Simpson, the backlog of work had kept him busy and he had little time for clock watching. Glancing at his watch, he noticed it was 1830 hours. Marty and the Chief had already 'cut a trail' and were homeward bound. If he was to meet Salazar, he'd have to wait until tomorrow to shuffle paperwork. He closed up shop by locking his file cabinet and was soon on his way.

It was 1900 hours sharp when he walked in the front doors of "The Perch Bar and Grill".

A friendly gray haired man met him with menu in hand.

"Welcome to The Perch. Would you be Mr. Simpson?"

"Yes."

"Please follow me." The gray haired man led Simpson down a well decorated hallway to the second door on the right. He gently knocked on the door and slowly opened it. "Sir, may I present Mr. Simpson." The man immediately turned and left the room and shut the door behind him. Now standing before Simpson was FBI Agent, Chris Salazar. He was every bit as Marty had described and more.

"Good evening, Detective Simpson. I'm very pleased to finally have the opportunity to meet you."

"The pleasure is mine, Agent Salazar. I can't help but notice you do keep meetings private!"

"It's an old habit of mine. Helps one stay alive in our line of work. I see they handed you a menu. May I say the steak and lobster is the way to go, of course with good vintage wine to whet the taste buds. By the way, the dinner is on me. Enjoy!"

In the beginning their conversation was very light and mostly about sports, in particular the Chicago Bears and Chicago Cubs. There seemed to be highs and lows in talking about teams past, present, and the dismal outlook for a Super Bowl win or a National Championship. Salazar's menu recommendations had been excellent. In the course of general conversation both men declared their single status in life and both preferred girls. That part was a great relief for Simpson since Salazar was truly the 'handsome dude' Marty had described.

"Simpson, since I called this meeting maybe it's time to get to the subject matter. I'm here because I need your help and the support of you entire department. Presently, I serve in Counter-Intelligence and we have a big problem. Likewise, I also recognize you have a similar problem. Simply put, who is the 'Wolf'? Frowning, Salazar continued.

"In order to move forward, let me share some insight with you. I'm certainly acquainted with your background and experience. I know you were brought into this case when Andrew Scoggins or what ever the hell his name is, was shot by a sniper. I also know you are familiar with the name Ann Duvall. We all need to know more about her.

"In addition, I have a very near friend, Helen a ex-FBI Agent. She now serves as an informant! Our relationship goes way back to our college days. At one time we really had the 'hots' for each other but it just didn't work out. Recently she let the 'cat out of the bag'.

Something big is going down in Seattle. I'll probably travel West to check things out!

"As my conversation was winding down with Helen, I asked her directly if she knew anything about the Wolf. Her reply was too quick. I can always tell when Helen is lying and that's one reason our relationship did not last. I'll be watching her like a hawk.

"I had occasion to talk with Lt. Harvell in Denver and he feels you may have additional information we need. Is it possible I have the right assumption? I need you to bring me up to date while we share and work together to stop this killing spree!"

Simpson smiling said. "I appreciate you calling this meeting because I believe it may be beneficial to this case."

Simpson recalled. "In the beginning, after the sniper incident, I sold my chief on allowing me to go it alone. I just felt I could obtain results faster. I was really wrong on this one!

This Andrew Scoggins is very good at what he does. It is becoming more apparent to me each day that Scoggins and the one we refer to as the Wolf are one in the same. My investigation in Denver comes out a big zero at this point. Another name popped up while in Littleton, Colorado, a Mr. Jack Abbott! Have you heard the name?" Before Salazar had a chance to answer, Simpson focused on Salazar's eyes and head movement.

"No, I don't remember hearing the name. Salazar lied! How does he fit into the picture?"

"At this point he doesn't!" Simpson's voice was firm in his delivery. Again, Simpson graded Salazar's reaction. "While checking a residence, a neighbor mentioned the name.

Sure you haven't heard the name before?" "No." he replied. Simpson now had doubts!

"While out West I did confirm, Andrew Scoggins and Ann Duvall are executives in International Oil & Gas. How much do you know about International Oil & Gas?" Simpson asked. Smiling, Salazar said, "Well, we know a little bit. It appears to be an active company and they did some drilling in Iraq. We have a man keeping us informed when there is activity in International's office in Denver."

"Is that Mr. Ivey? Simpson asked. A slight smile came across Salazar's face, "Could be."

"Salazar, who was the sniper who downed Andrew Scoggins?"

"You're getting down to the 'nut cutting' aren't you. I figured you'd get around to asking me before our meeting was over. Would you believe me if I told you, Kathy McBride? The same beauty who had you in her 'cross-hairs' before she met her assailant!"

"Who killed her?"

"A professional. We're still working on it! I have a question for you. Simpson are you going to Seattle?"

"No, I don't think so. I haven't asked since I've been out of the office for a while."

The two men shook hands and called it a day. In parting, Salazar waved and yelled, "Simpson, hope you change your mind about going to Seattle. We could use your help."

Chapter 18

Seattle, Washington.

The Wolf was now settled in at the Brown Hotel. He started re-organizing his operational plan. Strategically he had to become familiar with the Brown Hotel from basement to roof and all the floors in between, including offices, kitchen area, restrooms, janitor's area, utility closets, entries, and exits. Bottom line, he needed to know the hotel's operational procedures. One slip up or oversight could jeopardize the whole operation.

While considering all the facts, he had to come up with why the Cartels picked the Brown Hotel for their meeting. Why? Then it dawned on him, it was because of the waterways! Logic began to set in. First, the hotel was situated on the shoreline of Puget Sound. The waterways afforded immediate freedom if needed, as Puget Sound offered easy access to the, 'Strait of Juan De Fuca", gateway to the Pacific Ocean.

Suddenly, his cell phone rang. The screen started blinking while showing red as a signal the call was from the Attorney General, John Tatum. The number AG 1 appeared on the screen.

He answered his phone. "Yes sir."

"Your lair has been invaded! AG 2 will call you in three hours."

The message was loud and clear. Somebody was closing in on him. The person would have to be a professional because he had not left a trail. Maybe an informant had messed up by talking to the wrong person. The only two informants he was working with at this time were, Helen Schroeder, aka., Marie Higgins and Dave Snider, aka., Doug Taylor, her friend and sometime business associate.

For the present, he must consider the drug cartels who were gathering. The information he had gleaned indicated four cartels were involved with the possibility of a fifth to show.

Walking toward the hotel bar he encountered several men of Latin decent, each seemed friendly enough as they smiled or gave a nod of the head. It was shortly after 2140 hours and maybe they had a couple of scotch and waters and were feeling good. Anyway, there should be some loose talk in the bar area. The Wolf would be a good listener. He had just finished his first scotch and water when his cell phone sounded like a fire alarm. Hurriedly, he headed for the hotel lobby.

As he opened the cell phone, AG-2 appeared in bold print.

"Yes, I'm here."

"We have confirmed a severe leak in FBI Counter-Intelligence Division. The leak occurred in the Chicago Division. Several FBI agents are reported to be heading for Seattle! It is possible one of them was involved with the sniper you encountered. It is also likely one of them has connections with a cartel group!

"Report to AG-1 within forty-eight hours. Please confirm via text message."

He reacted immediately. Text message . . . . confirmed.

Now the Wolf's mind really ran rampant. His first thought was to locate the cartels assembling, then determine their logistic support systems, and how they were set up defensively.

It was important to know their strength in number, their weaponry, and their transportation to and from the hotel. He had to get organized and he needed help! It would be impossible for him to cover the entire operation; so he would depend heavily on Marie Higgins and Doug Taylor for assistance.

On second thought, he would empower Marie to look after Doug, since she was well acquainted with his temperament and his operational capabilities. In addition, somewhere in his cluttered mind, he would have to figure out how to recognize and cope with the FBI rogue agent.

The most important consideration was how to stay alive!

It now was 2018 hours he needed to get back to the scotch and water. As he seated himself midpoint at the bar, he heard loud laughter from two Hispanic males seated to his right. As the laughter subsided, he heard "Si, Jessie, you drive the fast boat."

"You talk about the Baja boat? She fast scooter!"

"Yeah man, we race to mother-ship, Lenora. I beat your ass at 60 miles per hour."

"No man, I need rest. Let's go to boats."

He had heard enough and would follow the two men to the hotel mooring dock.

Now he had it figured out. These two were employed by the cartels as boat coxswains.

As the two sailors staggered out of the hotel, he followed them to the docks. He was not surprised when the two men boarded their respective boats. They were tied side by side. It had been a long time since he had seen Baja 'Outlaw' Power Boats. These units were each sixteen feet in length, equipped for high performance, powered by 375 HP twin mercruiser inboard engines. The boats could easily cruise at sixty miles per hour with plenty of throttle left!

They would hold 185 gallons of fuel which would be ample supply to cruise the Strait of Juan De Fuca.

The Wolf watched intently as the two sailors throttled their boats to reverse positions to clear the docks.

Once the boats had made a safe turn out of the immediate dock area, the sailors opened up each boat's throttle and steered them toward open water in Puget Sound. It seemed as though the Wolf could hear the powerful boat engines for several miles out, as the boats raced toward the Lenora during the darkness of the night.

It had been a long day and it was time for him to return to his temporary lair, room #1016. As he opened his hotel door, he noticed the telephone light was blinking. He had received a call from Marie Higgins. He was somewhat inquisitive as to why she had not called his cell phone number, then he realized he had turned his phone off while following the two sailors. He immediately returned her call.

Marie was tired but she still had spunk in her voice. "Goodness me, you're keeping late hours."

"Marie, I'm sorry I'm so late in returning your call. I've been playing detective. Where are you located?

"I'm nearing Billings, Montana. Looking at my trusty map it appears I'm about eight-hundred miles from the Seattle area. How are your hotel accommodations?"

"Good. I've found us a couple of Baja high powered boats. Come on out and I'll take you for a fast boat ride."

"I'm peddling as fast as I can. Anything new happen?"

"Yeah, but it will have to wait until you arrive. Have you had any problems so far?"

"Sure have. Not to worry the problem was handled in a satisfactory manner. I'll give you a call in about fifteen hours, goodnight."

First thing come morning the Wolf needed to charter a helicopter. After seeing the two power boats he needed to find a ship, the Lenora!

Chapter 19

It was a beautiful day on Puget Sound. After a quick breakfast, the Wolf walked down to the dock mooring to check on the Baja boats. He viewed nothing but an empty pier. He remembered the two sailors talking about having a race. His assumption was the race was on toward the large ship, Lenora. The day seemed to be perfect and the sea water in Puget Sound gave off the 'fishy' odor. It reminded him of his Marine Corp days at Oceanside, California.

It was time to shake the memories and go to work.

When he returned to the hotel lobby, he asked the concierge to charter a helicopter for his use. He needed a pilot and helicopter usage for four hours. Time would be of the essence, and he would need the helicopter to be available within the hour. The concierge moved immediately and made the call. He handed the concierge a crisp one hundred dollar bill for services rendered.

When he arrived at the heliport, he had field glasses strapped around his neck and a 35mm camera in hand. The helicopter pilot was standing by the aircraft ready for his assignment.

The two men exchanged pleasantries and were air born within three minutes. While in the air he would take detail photos of the exterior of the Brown Hotel, adjacent parking lot, garage, and close-ups of the marina and boat moorings. He instructed the pilot to move down Puget Sound to the Shoreline area where he photographed the Melrose Hotel in like manner.

He would secure information from the pilot as to the distance from the Brown Hotel's docks to the entry of 'Strait of Juan De Fuca'. The pilot estimated the distance at ten miles. As they flew over Port Townsend and out into the Strait, the two Baja boats were running side by side and traveling northwest toward Pillar Point! As the helicopter flew over the boats, he took four photographs and thought he saw AK 47's laying on each of the front passenger seats.

When he returned to the hotel, he would take a closer look under his magnifying glass.

He immediately instructed the pilot to head to the Pillar Point, which was about ten miles northwest on the south side of the Strait. Since the weather had been cooperative and afforded good viewing, the pilot dropped his altitude to five hundred feet and headed northwest.

They were right on target. The ship, Lenora lay anchored two hundred yards off shore.

She was a beautiful white yacht flying the Spanish Flag. Both the pilot and Wolf estimated the yacht to be just under two-hundred feet in length. Again, he needed photos and he noticed eight deck hands scrubbing and cleaning the brass rails. Two of the crew members had removed canvas covers, brassily displaying fifty caliber machine guns mounted on the bow and stern of the ship. After the Wolf finished photographing the activity, he instructed the pilot to gain altitude up to two thousand feet and circle the ship for a few minutes. The wait was not long, without ten minutes the two Baja boats arrived and pulled along port side of the Lenora, **he** now had the confirmation he needed. The Lenora would be listed as his last major target!

The helicopter trip back to the heliport was uneventful; however the country side was beautiful.

Back at the Brown Hotel it was a busy morning. The lobby area was full of people hurrying around. At the check-out counters, five people were in the processing of paying their bills, while seven folks were trying to check-in. It seemed like excessive traffic to the Wolf. As he entered the elevator, he asked a bellboy if it was always this busy during a week-day.

"No sir, folks are coming in for the big Regatta this week-end. I think we're having about forty sailboats on Puget Sound Saturday. Then some will stay for sailing on Sunday."

On the surface the playing field was improving by the minute. A real festive mood was being set as multitudes of people would be scampering about. The large crowds would provide additional concealment and a certain amount of confusion as the action began. The only concern would be the collateral damage which might occur in the wake of his attacks.

It was time to examine his morning work. As he was viewing the photos of the Baja Power Boats, he confirmed the sailors aboard did have AK 47's laying in the front passenger seats. Turning to the yacht photos, the fifty caliber machine guns stuck out like sore thumbs.

In a short six hour period, he had identified a part of one of the cartels and confirmed they would be heavily armed. As he placed the photos in his luggage, he began to perspire heavily. He was familiar with the feeling and he knew the meaning! He had those feelings in both Nam and Iraq . . . he felt like he could smell death all around him. Within seventy-two hours, all hell was going to break loose in this peace abiding community. He had seen the results of fire-fights and bombings before and he had studied not only his adversaries but also the bystanders. Some would scream-out and freeze, while some would seek cover and try to fight back. Some would be killed or maimed for life; others would remember a terrible happening on this Regatta week-end.

It was lunch time and he decided to check out the Magnolia room. The menu posted on the billboard looked good and the price was right. The hostess seated him at a table near the entry way which gave him good opportunity to grade individuals as they entered the room. He was half way through his corn-beef sandwich when the hostess seated a stately gentlemen two tables to his right. The man was tall, slender, with cold black hair and a mustache well trimmed. He appeared to be Hispanic and had good command of both English and Spanish.

His waitress was Latino and they exchanged a couple of comments in Spanish and laughed. The man made a good impression and would be noticed in any crowd.

He continued to watch the man intently as he graded his behavior. One important point he noticed, the dark haired man took second looks at everybody who entered and left the room. It was obvious the man had special training in surveillance techniques. Suddenly, a heavy bearded Latino entered the room and was escorted to the man's table. The tall man stood up, shook the new comers hand and hugged him. Their conversation was not audible, yet he sensed they were talking business. Soon he exited the Magnolia Room and moved out into the lobby area where he would have a view when the two men left the room. For some reason this tall stately man looked familiar.

As the two men walked out of the restaurant, the man with the heavy beard handed the slender man an envelope and hurried out the front door of the hotel. The tall man moved to the hotel counter and said something to the hotel clerk and headed for the elevators. The Wolf followed and stepped in the elevator last. The tall man had pushed the eighth floor button.

With a pleasant smile he looked at the Wolf, "Which floor, sir?"

Seeming somewhat confused, the Wolf said, "Oh I'm sorry, I see you're going up to the eighth floor. I'm headed down for the parking garage. I'll catch the next elevator down."

This time he got a close up look at the man. There was absolutely no doubt in his mind now, he had seen this man before but he could not remember where or when.

It was time to go to work on identifying the cartels he was facing and their meeting place.

At this point he was confident he had pinpointed where these thugs would find lodging at night. It would not be the Brown Hotel. They were not taking chances since they had a floating sanctuary, the Lenora! For now he needed some inside help from one or two of the hotel employees. In most cases, a money hungry bellboy or the concierge would fit the bill.

While checking into the hotel, he had used fake identification showing current driver license, and passport as Jack Harris, Independent Oil Operator. He remembered the concierge was very attentive when he ordered the helicopter service. First choice, Henry Spencer, concierge extraordinaire! Entering the hotel lobby he walked over to Spencer's desk.

"Spencer good afternoon. I would like to buy you a beer this afternoon when you finish your days work. Would you have the time?"

"Sure would, Mr. Harris. I'll be off at six pm and we could go over to Tina's across the street.

The Wolf replied. "Sounds like a deal to me. See you at six.

A deal was made. Fixed cost at one hundred dollars a day for Spencer's assistance!

Chapter 20

A cool front had set in around the Chicago area; now a light mist had shrouded the Stoneliegh Apartment Complex and Ed Simpson could not sleep. He had way too much on his mind. Where were Andrew Scoggins and Ann Duvall? He dealt in logic, and people normally do not vanish into thin air. It was now 0400 hours, maybe a fresh cup of Maxwell House would help clear the cob-webs. From early morning until 0900, he re-lived his experiences in the Wolf case.

It was apparent he had overlooked an important lead and the USMC had not helped his frame of mind. In his office at 0930, he was looking over field notes he had made while in Denver; that's when Marty walked into his office with two sheets of paper and a big smile on her face.

"Good morning or afternoon, I've lost tract of time. You've got news from USMC's Administration Division!" Marty explained.

"Thank the Lord! Let me take a look." The USMC confirmed a Major Jack Abbott was honorably discharged from the Marine Corp. The USMC files showed no record on Andrew Scoggins. The Abbott information had been set-up by USMC and the Attorney General's office for top security reasons! Simpson would 'close file' on Jack Abbott! Simpson thought more about his special meeting with Chris Salazar, the handsome FBI Agent, who was also nipping at the heels of one Andrew Scoggins. The FBI must have a solid lead if the bureau was sending him to Seattle. Seems as though they would leave the investigation in Seattle up to the local boys. Maybe Salazar had not been so cooperative after all!

Simpson called Chief Turner on the intercom. "Chief we need to talk."

"Is it about girls?" Turner asked.

"No, it's about me."

"What a novel thought! Come on over." Turner replied.

"Chief, this Andrew Scoggins case is driving me up the wall. We received confirmation Major Jack Abbott was honorably discharged from USMC; then I found out he was killed in a drilling rig accident somewhere overseas. USMC does not have a file on Scoggins so I'm closing file on Jack Abbott! Something is up in Seattle and it leads me to believe it has to do with Scoggins, Duvall, and the Wolf. For some reason Salazar is going to Seattle and he indicated I could be of some help. What do you think?"

"I'm confident you could help out; however, I'll have a hard time selling the Mayor on such a project. When would you need to go out?" Chief Turner asked.

"I would need to be out there by Friday. There's going to be a lot of sailors in the area since they are having a regional regatta this coming week-end."

"Let me visit with the Mayor on this one. You are a helluva lot of trouble! I'll call you tonight and let you know. If the old man approves this one, you'll owe me another dinner."

After work, Simpson stopped at the Perch Bar and Grill for a couple of scotch and waters. While seated at the bar, it was time to relax and clear his mind. He glanced up at the mirror over the bar and caught a glimpse of Marty, his secretary, as she walked in the bar area. It didn't take long for him to leave the bar stool and head in her direction. He called out,"Marty over here".

Marty turned her head toward him, quicken her pace and held out a large manila envelope in front of him.

"I took a chance on finding you here. I'm glad I caught up with you before you've had too many. The chief wanted me to deliver this to you because you have to meet a timetable. You've got a plane to catch! In this envelope, there's Twenty-five hundred dollars, plus plane tickets. You have hotel reservations at the Brown Hotel in Seattle and you're cleared for late arrival. Can you swim?"

"Sure I can swim, why do you ask?"

"I over heard the Chief and the Mayor talking about you entering a Regatta!"

"My dear Marty, let me buy you a drink."

"Okay, only one. I've got to go grocery shopping."

The two employees of Chicago's finest enjoyed one drink together and they soon went their separate ways.

When Simpson boarded Frontier Flight # 356, he noticed a lot of folks were traveling West after regular working hours. He was seated on row twenty and was fortunate to be assigned an aisle seat. As the flight was air borne, he could not help but wonder why he was staying at the Brown Hotel. Chief Turner must have had a reason to have him booked at this particular hotel.

Maybe he had a late conversation with Chris Salazar or one of the other officers within the agency. After all it really didn't matter, he just felt lucky the Mayor approved his trip.

Chapter 21

It was 1730 hours as Helen Schroeder walked up to the front desk at the Melrose Hotel, Shoreline, Washington to check-in. This time she would register as Marie Higgins, CIA Agent Washington D.C. She carried fake driver license and passport reflecting same. The female clerk was friendly and asked the usual questions as to how long she would be staying, etc. It was moments like this her professionalism played a major role in accomplishing her objective. She asked to meet personally with the concierge. The hotel clerk made the introduction and Marie asked if they might speak in private. At this point, Marie Higgins produced her fake credentials and they were accepted by hotel management. Higgins pulled a bold move as she instructed the hotel staff to furnish her a complete listing of occupants every twelve hours.

The list would include check-ins and those who checked-out of the hotel. Higgins was smart enough not to require social security numbers, driver license numbers, or home addresses. By eliminating personal security information, she received full cooperation from the hotel staff.

Marie Higgins had just enough time to freshen up a bit before she was to meet Doug Taylor. She was anxious to learn more details so she could do some serious planning with the Wolf. When she stepped out of the elevator, she walked to the center of the lobby.

Looking around she spotted Taylor seated on a couch reading a late issue of Sports Illustrated.

"I would guess you are reading copy rather than eye balling the swim suit addition, right?"

Taylor looked up in total surprise. "You are a sneaky one aren't you? When did you get into town?"

"I believe it was a little after 1700 hours. How about you?"

"I came in late last night. Let's go across the street to the oyster bar. I'll treat you to a fine sea food meal," Doug suggested.

"Sounds like a deal to me. We've got a lot of catching up to do. You can start by telling me everything you know about what's coming down in beautiful Seattle!"

After the first round of Budweiser's, Doug Taylor began, "First let me say, we're up to our eyeballs with Drug Cartel operators, FBI Agents, CIA Agents, and local drug enforcement people, plus the Seattle Police Department and the Seattle Port Authority. To be honest it's kind of scary. I'm not sure we're going to be able to tell the good guys from the bad guys!"

Marie asked, "Who's your snitch on this one?"

"I have two in San Francisco and one here in Seattle. They are reliable! I'm going to have to ask the Wolf for some monetary funds on this one. I've been out three thousand bucks gathering information from these guys!"

Marie responded, "No problem, he'll reimburse you. Speaking of the man, have you contacted him?" Doug declared, "Not yet. I was waiting for you."

Brown Hotel 2120 Hours.

Battle plans were being assembled. The Wolf had listed the four Cartels attending this meeting. He had confirmed the Corzion Cartel out of Columbia had chartered the yacht, Lenora, her home port Lisbon, Portugal. Since the Corzion cartel and the Villarreal cartel worked hand in hand, it was likely Villarreal's Chief, Frank Cortez of Spain was either aboard ship or somewhere in the Seattle area. Just as he was laying out a 'flow chart' of the participates, his cell phone rang.

"Good evening, you big bad boy! Are you still 'huffing and puffing' to blow a house down? We're here and ready to meet. Are you available?" Higgins asked.

"Glad you made it before the party started. I'll meet you guys in the lobby. How long will it take you to get here?"

"We're at the Melrose. It will take about ten minutes if a taxi is outside. See you shortly."

The Wolf walked over to the concierge's desk. Henry Spencer, his new found assistant was no where to be found. He left a note for him to call at 2330 hours sharp.

When Marie Higgins and Doug Taylor walked into the hotel lobby, the Wolf glanced at his watch and it had taken them exactly ten minutes to reach the Brown Hotel. After the hugs and a kiss on Marie's cheek, he was ready to talk business. "Let's get a table in the bar area," he suggested.

The bar area was crowded but the threesome were able to find a table near the back of the room. The location would afford a certain measure of quietness which would allow them to hear each other speak.

The Wolf commented, "I do believe we have a few Latinos on the prowl this evening."

Doug responded, "Yeah, I've noticed but very few Senorita's. It sure would make the evening more enjoyable if we had a better mix!"

Smiling, Marie said, "Doug, you are incorrigible! Let's talk business. I've found out some of these male Latinos are sometimes hard to deal with. On the way out here, I had to fight off two hot blooded young men who had mucho to give! At least that was their claim to fame. I really didn't have the time or the desire to find out."

"I don't see any battle marks. What happened?" The Wolf inquired.

"It's really not worth talking about. They were drunk and I was lucky," Marie answered.

During their discussion, each described how they were registered in the hotels and the equipment to be used in the operation. The Wolf brought them up to date on his reconnaissance missions at the boat docks and his helicopter trip, while observing the Lenora. For tonight they would have a few drinks and observe the activities in hotel lobby area, bar, and boat docks. He felt certain the boat docks would be an active place, while the power boats would be transporting people to and from the ship, Lenora.

To set their plan in motion, Doug Taylor and Marie Higgins would move down to the docks and observe the power boat traffic. Meanwhile, he would stay close to the Concierge, Henry Spencer, to observe check-ins and those folks milling around the Brown Hotel lobby area.

One late arrival for lodging was Mr. Ed Simpson, Detective, Chicago Police Department.

The desk clerk motioned for Spencer to come to the check-in counter after Simpson headed for the elevators. The clerk handed a copy of the registration form to Spencer who immediately showed the information to the Wolf. Mr. Simpson had been assigned a room on the eleventh floor. Suddenly, the Wolf had total recall, the name Simpson rang a bell! It was the detective who had been on his tail in the Denver, Colorado area. Now he is in Seattle! How could he connect Andrew Scoggins to Jack Harris, it would have to be co-incidental. Or was it? Maybe he enjoys sailing and is here for the Regatta. On the other hand, maybe he is working closely with the FBI or the local agencies and possibly they have heard of a big cocaine shipment coming to Seattle.

It's a known fact, a lot of the drugs which enter the Seattle port, end up in the Chicago area.

Advantage Wolf! He knew what Mr. Simpson looked like and he knew his hotel room number. So far so good, Spencer was doing his job. Thus far the information gleaned would certainly be valuable to Marie Higgins. Sometimes it is truly amazing as to how people, and vital information fit together.

Approximately thirty minutes had past when FBI Agent, Chris Salazar approached the desk clerk and left a wake up call request for 0600 hours.

Spencer looking at Jack Harris asked, "Do you know him?"

Smiling, the Wolf responded. "No I saw him in the Magnolia Room earlier."

Spencer said. "That's Chris Salazar, FBI. I've watched him ever since he checked-in. He seems to be a real ladies man. He also enjoys riding in those Baja boats that Mr. Frank Cortez owns. Do you know Mr. Cortez? He's very wealthy and he comes from Spain!"

"Spencer you have just earned a bonus. I didn't realize you were a walking encyclopedia, how long have you known Mr. Cortez?"

With a faint smile, Spencer responded, "I guess about five years. Sometimes he sure brings good-looking women with him. Come to think about it, I can fix you up with one of his women."

"How much?"

"The good-looking ones will cost you five hundred for six hours," replied Spencer."

"Spencer you are a money making machine. How much is your cut?"

"No money. I can have a woman anytime I want her . . . all night free of charge."

Laughing, he said. "Spencer stay close to me. I may need you later."

He had made a lot of progress by being a good listener and by being at the right place at the right time. He watched Chris Salazar walk out of the hotel toward the boat docks.

Chapter 22

The Wolf canceled his 2330 appointment with Spencer. He decided he would have a couple of scotch and waters before retiring to his room. On entering the bar area, he saw Ed Simpson seated at a table by himself. He decided to test the waters!

"Good evening, I'm Jack Harris. I was in the lobby when you checked-in. May I join you as I hate to drink alone. Hopefully I'm not being pushy."

"Not at all. I feel the same way when I'm traveling. I'm Ed Simpson, have a seat."

When the waitress appeared, the Wolf ordered Chivas Regal Scotch.

"Well, I see you know what to order," Simpson remarked.

"It's seldom I drink, but when I do, I always try to order the best."

"Jack, what brings you to the beautiful city of Seattle?" Simpson inquired.

"Boats. I think sailboats are beautiful to watch, but the way these sailors are able to traverse and tact, sending their boats in different directions is truly amazing."

Looking directly at Simpson, Jack asked. "How about you Mr. Simpson, have you mastered the art of sailing?"

Taking another sip of scotch, Simpson replied. "No way. About the only sailing I've done is when I was a kid I sailed a small model boat in mom's fish pond. But like you, I do enjoy watching them sail in regattas.

"I'm here on business, but I think I'll take the opportunity to watch the Regatta this week-end and then travel on to Victoria, British Colombia."

Smiling, the Wolf asked, "Have you been there before?"

"No, but I hear it's beautiful country." Simpson answered.

"You hit the nail right on the head. May I suggest you visit the Buchart Gardens. You will always remember the trip. They are very special."

"Jack you must travel a great deal. What do you do for a living?"

"I deal in Oil and Gas properties."

The remark grabbed Simpson's attention. "Have you been in military service?"

"Yeah, I had a tour of duty in Nam and Iraq before taking on the oil and gas business."

Simpson said. "Let me order us another round of drinks. Then he asked, which branch of service?"

"Only if you will allow me to buy. Marine Corp," replied the Wolf.

"Nothing doing. I'll put this one on my expense statement. My boss always enjoys catching my excessive spending. For some reason, he always thinks a woman is involved", smiling, Simpson replied.

"Mr. Simpson, I appreciate your hospitality. I hope I'll be able to reciprocate."

"Tell me about your Marine Corp experiences. And by the way just call me Ed! I enjoy meeting service men. I had a short stay in 'Nam as an airplane mechanic."

"Okay, Ed. I appreciate what you have said. I've always felt honored to be able to answer the call of my country. I'll share an item or two with you as we finish our drinks. I somewhat have empathy for the guys in the Korean conflict and those of us who served in Nam. If you're going to fight a war, then I think we should fight to win!"

"I could not agree more. I believe you also mentioned you served in Iraq. Is that correct?"

"Yes I did."

"May I ask, in which units did you serve?" Simpson inquired.

"Reconnaissance Companies both tours!"

Simpson smiling," I had a friend named Jack Abbott who served in Iraq. Did you happen to know him?"

"Sorry Ed, I did not know him; however, it's interesting you mention the name. Recently, I was in Denver, Colorado. As I was checking into the Hilton Hotel on South Colorado Boulevard, I distinctly heard the Concierge page Jack Abbott. When you mentioned that name, I knew I had heard it before!"

"Are you serious?" Simpson asked.

"Yes, I'm sure! I'm confident the page was for Jack Abbott," he said firmly."

"Mr. Harris, if you will excuse me, I need to go to my room and make a phone call."

Smiling the Wolf said."Absolutely no problem. Hope to see you tomorrow and I'll buy the drinks."

As Simpson paid the bar cashier, he noticed three Latinos from two tables over follow Simpson to the elevators. It was obvious the three men were about to 'roll' Simpson for his money ; or they had learned he was a detective from Chicago. In his opinion both assumptions meant real trouble. As he watched the elevator ascend to the eleventh floor, he knew if he was going to help Simpson he had to make a move. Quickly he punched in the eleventh floor on the adjacent elevator. At this juncture, there was absolutely no time to think about his own safety; it was time to go into action and save a detective from harms way. After all, Simpson was from Chicago and he liked the Chicago Bears!

The Wolf pulled his 9mm Glock and cocked the hammer back. When the elevator doors opened on the eleventh floor, he saw the three men had Simpson facing the wall with his back to the elevators. One of the Latinos had a 45 Caliber pistol pointed at Simpson's head, one man held a stiletto knife in his right hand, while the other man held Simpson's wallet in his left hand and was cursing Simpson for being a detective after their drugs!

The Wolf fired three rapid rounds from his 9mm Glock.

The first round hit the man with the 45 Caliber pistol directly in the back of his head, splattering skull bone fragments over Simpson's shoulders. The second round hit the assailant holding the stiletto between his shoulder blades, entering his chest cavity severely damaging the left lung and heart. The third assailant dropped Simpson's billfold, while turning toward the Wolf. His third round found it's mark, center forehead and the man's head literally exploded. Three men lay dead at Simpson's feet. The kills took less than twelve seconds. Detective Ed Simpson was safe; however, he was in a state of shock and could not identify his benefactor!

Before Simpson could turn toward the elevator, the Wolf dropped a silver wolf signet on the carpet outside the elevator and immediately entered the stairway. Once inside the stairway, he quickly headed down to the tenth floor. For the next few hours, his room would serve as a place of refuge. He knew his actions would leave Ed Simpson confused and bewildered, while local authorities tried to figure out what in the hell took place in the hallway on the eleventh floor.

The Wolf called Marie on her cell phone to confirm their scheduled meeting.

Marie and Doug Taylor knew something was going on because the local police department arrived in full force, with ambulances and a SWAT Team for additional support. He told her he would explain during their meeting. She told the Wolf their team had set up surveillance at a sidewalk cafe near the boat docks and she had the Baja Power Boats in full view. Both she and Doug would come to his room at 2330 hours.

Sometimes 'stakeouts' are boring and time passes very slowly. Both members of this surveillance team were professionals and knew how to pass the time away. Since they were seated at separate tables and could not converse, they spent their time watching and grading individuals as they passed their tables. Suddenly, Marie Higgins motioned for Doug to join her table. This move was somewhat out of character. As Doug approached her table, he could see she had turned white as a sheet and was shaking like a leaf.

"Lady, what in the hell's the matter with you? Have you seen a ghost?"

"Doug, hold me for just a minute!"

As he pulled Marie close, he felt a tear on her right cheek. "Why are you crying?"

"Doug, I've seen a dear friend with two Latinos, and they are walking out on the dock to get in one of those Baja boats!"

"Who is this friend?" Doug asked.

Wiping away a tear, Marie said. "His name is, Chris Salazar and he is a special friend."

"When and where did you know this man?"

Looking toward the boat, Marie confided, "It's a long story and it's very personal. This is a bad deal! I've got to talk to the Wolf."

"Marie, we're operating as a team. Tell me exactly what you're talking about. Who is this man and why does this mean trouble?"

"Doug, this man is an FBI Agent out of Chicago! I've got to find out what he is doing with people associated with the drug cartels!"

Chapter 23

Corporal Dorrance Statton of the Seattle Police Department knocked on the door of Room #1016. The knock was loud and sounded authoritative. The Wolf peered through the security peep hole and opened the door.

"Sir, I'm checking out this floor for security reasons. We've had a shooting on the eleventh floor. Have you left your room in the last hour? Statton asked.

"No sir, I've been watching the Chicago Cubs baseball game. The Rangers are leading 2-1, and it's the bottom of the eighth!"

Corporal Statton replied, "I hope those Rangers beat their ass. Did you hear any shots being fired?"

"Officer, I'm afraid not. I had my head buried in the television set, with the volume up high. This hotel has done a good job with the sound proofing. Sorry, I don't think I can help you much. If you don't mind me asking, was anyone hurt?"

"Yeah, some bastard 'popped' three Latinos and it didn't take long for him or her to do the job. Three shots were fired and we've got three bodies. Somebody's good at rapid fire!" Officer Statton looked somewhat bewildered as though he didn't know what to do next.

"Here, take my card and please report to the hotel security office if you see or hear anything you consider suspicious."

"Officer Statton, I'll be happy to cooperate with your department."

Statton turned to the door across the hall to continue his investigation.

The Wolf's cell phone rang.

"We've got to talk. Is it okay if we come on up? I know we're a little early for our scheduled meeting, but I've had a major development," Higgins explained.

"Wait about thirty minutes before you come up. I've had a visitor. The police are checking out this floor since the shooting on the eleventh!"

"We knew something major had happened in the hotel. Have you been on the prowl?"

"Yes, but not intentionally. I helped out a drinking buddy in time of need," The Wolf explained. After hanging up her cell phone, Marie and Doug headed for the hotel coffee shop. Entering the hotel lobby they viewed eight police officers milling around.

Higgins turning to Taylor said, "Now I see what the Wolf was talking about. We'll have to take our time in the coffee shop and chit chat for a while. Maybe I can recover from my shock and share in more detail regarding my sighting.

"Doug, I just can't believe what I saw! I have a very dear friend who's high up in the FBI and serves in the Chicago office. We go way back to college days and at one time I thought I was in love with him. Best said, it just didn't work out. In the past he has been my help-mate on several cases and I have always thought he was on the up and up, but now I have serious doubts. I've got to relate the details to the Wolf. This turn of events could put this whole operation in jeopardy. To say the least somebody could be hurt."

Doug asked, "Do you still have strong feelings for this individual?"

"Doug, I still care for him. I'm not in love with him, but I consider him a friend."

"Could you terminate him if necessary?"

"I pray it will never come to that," Marie responded.

Doug said in a very firm voice,"Well, I agree we've got to share every detail with the Wolf. It may be he'll call you off this operation. You're professional and you realize we cannot let personal feeling intervene in a time of crisis." Marie Higgins begin to sob, "I understand."

When Doug and Marie knocked on the door of room #1016, they heard the Wolf say, "I need a password. I don't allow just anyone to enter my lair!"

"How about I'll blown your house down," said Marie.

Laughing, the Wolf said,"I can't allow that to happen! I've got to protect my fat little pigs. Come on in."

The minute Marie Higgins entered the room, he could tell she had been crying. The laughter subsided and a frown came across his face. Looking directly into

Marie's eyes he asked, "Young Lady why have you been crying?"

"It's a Lady thing," Marie responded. Doug Taylor wouldn't let it go,"It's more than that, and we've all got to talk!" The Wolf led Marie to a comfort chair and seated her."Okay, Marie let's out with it!"

"I really don't know where to start. It's a long story and it goes back to my college days. Years ago I met a man by the name of Chris Salazar and we thought we were in love; however, it didn't work out but we've remained friends ever since. As a matter of fact we worked together on several occasions when I was with the FBI. Chris Salazar is currently an FBI Agent stationed in the Chicago District Office. I have visited with him from time to time, strictly on a platonic relationship basis." Wolf with a slight smile. "How long has it been since you have visited with him?"

Marie, wiping her right cheek with a handkerchief, "It's been approximately three weeks. Best I recall, I believe it was about the time you were finishing up your assignment in St. Louis. He came to my apartment and I fixed dinner." Looking directly into Marie's eyes, the Wolf asked, "Did you tell him you were coming to Seattle?"

"No, not intentionally. I had some material, maps, etc. of Seattle laying on my kitchen bureau. He may have gotten a glimpse of those, I don't know. I certainly did not relate to him I was working a deal in Seattle!"

Doug Taylor requested, "Tell me what this guy looks like. I think it would take someone outstanding to gain you attention. I've been trying for years and you barely recognize I exist."

"Doug, I'm sorry I didn't know."

"Okay, you guys knock it off! We've got a lot to think about here," the Wolf bellowed.

The Wolf asked. "Marie, I know you well enough to know you are professional. How far can you go if called upon? Will you be able to terminate this individual if it is necessary? I pray to our God we'll never have to make that decision, but I must know where you stand!"

"I'll not let you down," Marie responded.

By this time Doug Taylor was exasperated, he had not had a reply from Marie regarding Salazar's appearance.

"May I ask Marie one more time about this man's appearance? Down at the docks I thought she had seen a ghost, or some terrible figure which had scared the daylights out of her." Doug, I for one appreciate your tenaciousness. You do need to know. I guess I was too anxious to find out if she could perform under these unusual circumstances. I preempted your inquiry. Marie, would you like to describe Salazar?"

"Well Doug. In lady's terms, he is a very handsome man. Tall, slender, with piercing brown eyes, black hair and mustache. I might quickly add, he has a way with the lady folks. As far as I know, he has never been married and he lives off the fat of the land.

Hopefully, that statement will describe his modus operandi."

"I believe I get the picture." Doug replied.

For over two hours, the three met and drew up their preliminary battle plan against the four drug cartels. Come morning the helicopter would be leased for the days activity. Marie and Doug would pick up the Wolf at exactly 0800 and take close inventory on the arsenal Marie had brought with her as a support system. Shortly after, they would fly by helicopter to Pillar Point to take another close look at the Lenora. It had been determined they would need a rubber boat and diving gear for close work on the Lenora, since the Wolf would not allow the ship to sail from the Strait of Juan De Fuca!

Chapter 24

Ed Simpson was beginning to feel like a criminal. Usually, he was the one asking the questions; but now, he was the subject of an investigation by the Seattle Police Department, FBI, and CIA officials. He was having a very difficult time explaining how three Latinos lay dead at his feet. Maybe there is some truth in who you might know, rather than how much you know.

Chris Salazar entered the interrogation room!

"Ed, what the hell is going on? I left you in Chicago and you told me you were not coming to Seattle."

Smiling. "Well, I got uneasy. I knew you were coming out and I didn't want you to receive all the credit for capturing the Wolf!"

"Okay, my good friend let's dispense with all the crap. Tell me exactly what happened."

"It's kind of a long story but I'll try to remember. After I checked-in, I was tired and a little lonely so I headed for the bar. I was drinking alone and a man asked if he could join me.

He seemed like a nice guy, so we had a few drinks together."

"Then what happened?," Salazar asked.

"I think he told me he was from Chicago and he was in the oil and gas business. To be honest, I was drinking heavy shots of scotch. It didn't take long for the scotch to hit me hard. I can't remember much after that," Simpson replied.

"Look, Ed we've got a real problem here. You really need to remember who you were drinking with and how three men ended up murdered in cold blood at your feet."

"For the life of me, I'm blank! All I remember is getting off the elevator and some guys pushed me against the wall and were 'rolling me'. They had my wallet and were screaming at me. I do remember one had a .45 Colt pointed at my head. Damn, the bore of that piece looked like a cannon!"

"You 'flatfoot'! What if I told you the Wolf was a part of this action. What would you think about that?" Chris Salazar inquired.

"What are you talking about?" Simpson asked.

"Just what I said. Since you are from Chicago, I'll repeat it! It is likely you encountered the Wolf in the hallway of the eleventh floor. Our men found a wolf signet laying on the carpet near where the men lay dead. It is apparent for the first time, the Wolf became a good Samaritan rather than an out and out murderer! Ed, you are a lucky man to be with us today," Salazar said frowning.

Shaking his head, Ed said, "'Thanks for bringing me up to date. Is it okay with you people if I try to grab a little shut-eye? It's been a long night."

"Fine, we'll need to visit again when you've cleared your head. It is extremely important for you to remember your drinking buddy's name last night. He could be our man!"

Shaking his head back and forth, Simpson said. "Are you trying to tell me, I may have been drinking scotch with the Wolf while in the hotel bar?"

"You got it pal," replied Salazar.

As Ed Simpson was entering the elevator, Doug Taylor held the elevator door open for Marie Higgins to step out into the lobby area. Both Marie and Doug acknowledged a 'good-evening' to Simpson as they stepped out. It had been a busy day and all parties needed a good night's rest. Sometimes lives cross paths without the individual parties recognizing the significance of the encounter. This night was one of those occasions. In less than forty-eight hours they would meet again under totally different circumstances!

The Wolf was lying in bed wide awake, while reminiscing about the days activities and considering the scope of this assignment. What would the morning bring? His thoughts were centered around the enormous task the good guys faced in the sinking of the Lenora. At that moment his cell phone rang. The screen again was red and reflected the call was from AG-7! He started not to answer the call, but felt it must be important. Since it was 0200 hours Pacific Standard Time, he felt compelled to answer it. He opened the cell phone.

"Yes!"

A very nice sounding lady's voice said, "Early this morning AG-1 instructed me to contact you. I'm sorry about the time difference, but I was instructed to call you immediately. I have been ordered to join your party!"

Wide eyed, the Wolf said,"Lady, I don't know who in the hell you are, or how you secured my phone number. Give me a call back number and you'd better be for real."

Suddenly the phone line went open. The Wolf immediately hit his recall button on the cell phone with no response. Within twenty seconds he was sent a text message in morse code, listing name, agent number and phone number. Now fully awake maybe he could make sense out of the early morning call. He punched in the new number. The good sounding female voice answered.

"Good morning. I'm truly sorry about awakening you this morning. I'll make sure it doesn't happen again."

"Please verify your name again."

"I'm Special Agent, Gloria Hampton. I report directly to the Attorney General's office. I served as Colonel in the USMC Intelligence Division with classification 0231. I'm cleared for 'Most Secret'. I have recently finished my assignment with the Treasury

Department and I'm ready to report for duty. It is my understanding you could use a good soldier. Is that right?"

"Do you have a specialty?"

"Yes, I kill bad people! Will you pick me up at the Seattle Airport at 0930?"

"I will. Give me some ID."

"I'll be dressed in marine drab uniform. I have auburn hair and I'm five foot nine inches in marine corp dress heels. I'm arriving on a military flight; however, I'll be shuttled by government vehicle to concourse # 22, gate # 8. How will I recognize you?"

He responded. "You won't. Don't be late!"

Chapter 25

At exactly 0700 the Wolf called Marie Higgins and informed her the game plan had been changed and they had a new member of the team joining them at 0900. He would try to explain the changes on their way to the Seattle Airport. Just to show a little 'Semper Fi', he dressed in a faded pair of marine corp dungarees. The green denim cloth felt good, while the 'look' should make, Colonel Gloria Hampton feel welcome and among friends.

The drive to the airport seemed like time well spent. Both Marie and Doug asked a lot of questions he could not answer due to confidentiality, or the fact he didn't have a clue as to the correct answer. Like, why is

Colonel Gloria Hampton joining the team at this late date? The Wolf figured only two people knew the answer to that one. The Attorney General and Colonel Hampton. Marie Higgins parked her car on the second floor of the parking garage which afforded some cover from the passing traffic. The facility was not well lighted and allowed them the opportunity to move about while checking the arsenal Marie had packed. The Wolf headed for concourse # 22, gate #8. As usual the airport was extremely busy with folks from all walks of life trying to get from here to there. Near the gate, the 'Gateway News Stand' made an ideal place to loiter for a while until Colonel Hampton made her appearance on Concourse #22.

At promptly 0925 hours the airport paging system kicked in and Colonel Gloria Hampton received a page. The Wolf froze! The question raced across his mind. Was he being set-up? The page announcer requested Colonel Hampton report to the Northwest Airline Ticket Counter on Concourse #22. The airport announcer paged her again at 0928 hours. He moved away from the news stand so he could view the Northwest ticket counter. Time was moving rapidly as he watched intently for five minutes. Colonel Hampton did not make an appearance.

Slowly turning his head to the right he caught a glimpse of her as she pulled her travel cart onto the ground escalator. Now she was firmly in his sight and he liked what he saw! Immediately he situated himself next to the wall so she would have to walk in front of him to pass. He walked briskly to catch up with her. As he stepped beside her, he gently placed his left hand on her right forearm. She quickly glanced over toward him, he smiled and handed her a wolf signet. She stopped abruptly and asked. "What's your real first name?" With a very serious look he replied. "Jack" Colonel Hampton said, "Good to meet you Jack, let's get out of this busy airport."

"For the sake of time in getting better acquainted, I'm going to call you Gloria, okay?"

Gloria smiling. "It's a done deal."

"Gloria, I forgot to mention you were paged twice before your arrival. You are suppose to report to the Northwest Airlines Ticket Counter."

With a faint smile,"That's okay it was my brother. He thought I was coming in on "Northwest Airlines. I'll return his call later. Thanks for telling me."

For the time being the Wolf accepted her reply. He put the item on a mental hanger to remember he would like to meet 'brother' in the near future.

By the time they reached the parking facility, the Wolf was pulling the travel cart and was feeling good the Attorney General had enough fore thought to send him help. After all he could have assigned some ugly old boy with hair on his legs. Now he just hoped his other warriors would feel good about the Colonel. The introductions were handled in a formal way.

Upon meeting Colonel Gloria Hampton, Doug Taylor, aka, David Snider was happy as a lark. He had high hopes he would be working right along side her all the way. The Wolf was having a hard time diagnosing Marie Higgins feelings. He knew for certain sometimes ladies have to go through adjustment periods and sometimes it takes a while. Marie went to work immediately on checking Gloria's credentials by asking what seemed like a hundred questions.

At least the 'claws' were not showing on either party and the Wolf took it as a good sign. After picking up an Avis car rental they were soon on their way. The other folks in the group had no idea he was familiar with the territory. As a young marine officer he and his wife, Connie had visited this area on several occasions before they had children. For now he would try to keep his mind on his work. He called the heliport and asked the pilot to pick his group up at 1400 hours at the Henry Blake Lighthouse near Sequim.

On their way to Pillar Point most of the time was spent briefing Gloria Hampton. Surprisingly, she knew more than they thought she did. The truth be known, Gloria Hampton had studied complete background checks on all parties. She had given extra consideration to the Wolf. She knew Jack Abbott's history from birth, high school, college days and all the way through his war time service records. She knew his wounds, medals, etc. All that was missing were the details on Connie Abbott, Evelyn's and Michael's deaths! She knew they were killed in an automobile accident, but she had no way of knowing how devastating their loss was to Jack Abbott.

While he continued to drive Highway 112, the Wolf related a great deal of history regarding the territory between the Olympic Mountains and the Strait of Juan De Fuca. A plain area which afforded the Klallam Indians,(Strong People), sufficient range for their tribes to survive. He was drawing on previous knowledge obtained when he and Connie were together.

Since both were history buffs, it made travel interesting back in those days. In several ways it was good for him to have time to reminisce. For a few hours it would take his mind off killing.

He needed that! He was beginning to have a good feeling toward Gloria. It seemed she just fit right in and he was very comfortable with her in his presence. At this point he had concerns about Marie and Gloria getting along. Knowing Marie's temperament, he knew she would not put up with someone who was 'a know it all'. With her FBI background and the special training she had received it could be a 'stand-off' between the two ladies. So far so good!

Chapter 26

Aboard the Lenora Yacht 1100 hrs.

In the Captain's meeting room, Chris Salazar stood before four Drug Cartel Kingpins and their operational officers. Each Cartel had sufficient representation in order to set time tables, establish responsibilities for each in the areas of security, procurement of drugs, prostitutes, and logistical support for the entire operation. This 'job' was for only professionals and would be an enormous opportunity for the four Cartels to make over five billion dollars. FBI Agent, Chris Salazar stood to gain three million bucks to his part. His rogue mindset led him to believe it would be a good pay-day for an agent gone bad! He planned to retire immediately, take his three million in cash and head for Columbia. With that kind of money, he felt he could live a lavish life style, chase women and drink good booze the remainder of his life.

Salazar, knew first hand, he was not dealing with novices and that Frank Cortez who headed the Villarreal Cartel had to be handled with kid gloves. Cortez had a killer instinct and was noted for being unforgiving. If one of his henchmen messed up an assignment he would be eliminated immediately. His reputation was well recognized by Salazar and other members of the Cartels. On the other side of the coin, Juan Corzion was easy going and trusted his men. He had a big ego and thoroughly enjoyed the company of good-looking women. The women under his command were well educated but had enormous appetites to make big money; consequently they would perform as ordered. The daily orders were to sexually satisfy him and his associates as needed. In addition, the other Cartels represented were the Sinaloa Cartel serving the Guadalajara and Ciudad Juarez area, while the Zeta Cartel would serve Guerrero, Moreles, Nuevo Leon, Mexico City, Coahulia, and Chihuahua areas. For this very special peaceful meeting all wars would be put aside for the time being. When it came to big bucks, their disagreements could be temporarily laid aside and they would enjoy the whores and the tequila at every opportunity.

Frank Cortez considered free drugs and sex as fringe benefits.

At 1300 hours one of the Baja Power Boats pulled along port side of the Lenora. The Captain of the Lenora welcomed aboard three representatives of the Thailand Global Horizon's Recruiters. They were immediately taken to the Cartel meeting. At this moment all the power players were aboard the Lenora. The Wolf had word that there was the possibility five cartels would be meeting. His informant had considered the Thailand group as the fifth cartel. At this point he had not been informed of their arrival. As to the makeup of those in attendance, it really didn't matter to him. His main focus would be to rid the World of these thugs who would inflict pain and suffering on innocent people! For the next few hours they would be occupied in big business planning; after which, it would be fun and games. Frank Cortez greeted the Thailand Group with a 'Saludos'! He raised his glass to the three men who would bring young whores to be shipped to the United States."Mucho Dinero", he declared!

The Cartels initial meeting would last until 1340 hours; then the Ship's bar would be open and the whores aboard would be brought in to mingle with the crowd. The Lenora's amenities were adequate to serve the crowd.

Chris Salazar made a quick phone call to his superior officer in Chicago to let him know he was working on behalf of the United States Government. He had Frank Cortez in his sights so to speak. All was well, and going as planned. With a little luck he would finish his job by the week-end. Salazar knew how to play both ends against the middle as he 'stroked' his boss. Over the years in service he had developed a demeanor which was difficult to define. People who had known him for years were not any better acquainted with him than they were on the first day they met. However, he had such a pleasing personality most people wanted to be in his company.

Smiling, Frank Cortez approached Salazar.

"Chris, I want you to come to my cabin. I have a woman for you. Her name is Loretta and she is from Spain. I have not had her yet. I give her to you. She was standing on the Bridge of the Lenora when you arrived on the boat. She likes you. She asked me to bring you to her!"

Salazar frowning, "Oh Frank, I have to wait. I just finished talking to my Chicago office. I must go into Seattle immediately. I was about to ask a favor of you. I need for one of your Baja boat crews to take me to the main land as soon as possible. "Would you do that for me?"

With a glass of tequila in his right hand and his left arm around Salazar's shoulder he said. "My dear friend, what is mine is yours. Yes, we go. I will go with you and we will bring our sweet little Loretta with us." Frank called to his Captain, "Make ready a Baja Boat, several of us are going to Seattle!" Frank Cortez was not lying about the beautiful, Loretta! Before the cartels adjourned their meeting, Chris Salazar had one more topic to discuss. Standing before the group once again, he needed to warn his comrades of the impending danger they were facing while in Seattle.

"Senors, I have information to share so listen very carefully. Today, we have had a good meeting and agreements have been reached regarding operational responsibilities for each cartel including assigned territories and logistics. One item I have not covered with you . . . maybe you have heard of the Lobo! In America, we call him the Wolf. This man is a trained killer and he is in our area. It seems for some reason he has declared War on my amigos! Do not take this man lightly. Last evening he 'popped' three of Frank Cortez's men at the Brown Hotel. He leaves a 'calling card', a silver signet of a Wolf. As yet, some of you have not gone to port in Seattle. When you dock in Seattle use caution because this is his hunting ground. Any questions?"

One of the Sinaloa Cartel members asked, "He like nina's? We have many small girls we give him!"

"Senor, hide your girls. If you make such an offer he will kill you," replied Salazar.

"He mean Hombre, yes? We kill the Lobo!"

At 1450 hours the Baja power boat pulled along the port side of the Lenora and began loading members of the cartels, plus the Thailand support group. For now it would be considered 'shore leave' time for fun and games.

Chapter 27

The 'Chopper' landed at Sequim at exactly 1410 hrs., destination Pillar Point. Flying along the south coast of the Strait of Juan de Fuca, the Wolf and his associates spotted the two Baja power boats traveling northeast toward Puget Sound. At this point he ordered the 'Chopper' pilot to set down at Pillar Point. The group would need thirty minutes to pick up diving gear and rent a boat for a 'special job', the sinking of the Lenora!

Immediately after the quick shopping spree, it was on to observe the Lenora crew in attendance, positioning offshore, and more photographs. It was at this point when

Gloria asked, "Do we have to send this beautiful ship to Davy Jone's Locker?"

"Yeah, that's what I want to know too. Why don't we just consider her a government issue and sail her down to Argentina for about six months?" Marie said laughing.

Smiling, the Wolf asked Doug, "How about it Doug? You know anything about ships?"

"You bet your ass I do. After four years with Uncle Sam aboard the Menard, I know how to 'chip' paint and re-paint!" Doug replied.

The Wolf asked the pilot to take one more fly-over the Lenora, with a serious look on his face the Wolf asked, "Gloria do you have all the photos of the Lenora you need?"

Frowning Gloria answered, "Yes, but I still hate to think about sending her to the bottom.

Likewise, I'm concerned about those two machine guns facing the bow and the stern.

Based on my experience, I believe those are going to have to be neutralized as we come aboard! Looking at the Wolf, how do you plan to do that?"

Smiling, he said, "Well, we all have our little opportunities . . . I was planning on letting Doug handle those at his convenience!"

"Consider it done my friend. I think Marie packed a 155 Howitzer somewhere in the trunk of the nifty Ford she drove out here." The group had a chuckle over the remark; however, before long all the smiles would disappear as life and death will be the issue!

On the return trip to Seattle, Marie would recount her experience with Chris Salazar for Gloria's benefit. She went back to the beginning. To everybody's surprise Gloria had heard about Chris Salazar from the Justice Department. She was surprised to learn of his direct association with the Cartels.

When they arrived in the Seattle area, it was decided to leave Marie's Ford at the airport and they would continue to use the Avis Rental Car. With the additional diving gear, it was now necessary to transfer all the gear to the rental unit, and use the helicopter when needed. It would be a quick dinner at the Oyster Bar and then make contact with some of the members of the Cartels.

It didn't take long for the Cartel members to show their brassy behavior along dock-side as the power boat pulled into dock. The 'cat-calls' were frequent as the members called to the girls along the sidewalk cafes.

Simpson happened to be standing near the guard rail at the Oyster Bar when one of the Lenora sailors grabbed a waitress by the arm and pulled her close, yelling mucho, mucho! Ed stepped in between the two of them.

With a scowl on his face, Ed yelled, "Com padre, ha llegado la policia!"

Momentarily, the sailor looked confused as though he certainly was not expecting a police officer to be at hand. He stepped back and smiled and gave Simpson a sign by extending his right hand and lifting his middle finger. Simpson pulled his handcuffs and was about to 'cuff' the sailor, when one of the sailors shipmates pulled him back from the railing and pushed the shipmate toward the walkway.

Smiling, the shipmate offered an apology for his friend. "Tengo que pedirte perdon."

Simpson, with a slight grin, "Apology accepted."

Dark had set in by the time the foursome had arrived at the Baker Hotel. As they entered the lobby area, the Wolf's on site informant, Henry Spencer, spotted him as he approached the elevators.

"Mr. Harris do you have a minute?"

Excusing himself from his group, he walked over to Spencer. "What's up?"

"We've got some new arrivals," explained Spencer.

Smiling, the Wolf asked, "Like who?"

"The big man himself, Frank Cortez, and he has brought some beauties with him! Do you need a woman for tonight?

"Spencer, you are an okay guy. Thanks for asking but I'm okay. Handing Spencer a crisp one hundred dollar bill, by the way do you have room numbers for your new arrivals?".

"Yes sir, it's the penthouse all the way. The whole 16th floor and there's some good-lookers with his party! May I ask who are your lady friends? I'd like to meet the tall one."

"Believe me, Spencer you couldn't handle the Lady"

With a big grin on his face he whispered, "I'd sure like to try."

With an inquisitive look, the Wolf asked. "Spencer, what time do you go off duty?"

"Why?" Spencer asked.

"Oh, you look tired. I want you to get plenty of rest. I may need you tomorrow evening."

"Mr. Harris, I won't be able to help you tomorrow or the next day. You remember the Regatta starts tomorrow morning at 1000 hours."

"That's right Spencer. I've got the oil business on my mind and I just forgot. You take it easy for the next couple of days."

"Okay, Mr. Harris. If you need anything at all just leave word at the front desk and I'll make sure you receive good service."

When the Wolf and his group reached his room, he informed them about Frank Cortez and his people occupying the Penthouse on the sixteenth floor. He would step up the attack schedule after learning he had a suitable target!

"Marie, it's time to move out! You and Doug retrieve the other firearms you left in your Ford located on airport premises. If you packed 12 gauge assault shotguns with .00 buck bring two of those. Likewise, I believe we're going to need at least four smoke grenades.

Are these items available?"

With a slight grin, Marie responded, "That and more if needed!"

"It is essential the element of surprise be employed if we are to nullify the use of their AK 47's. While you and Doug are retrieving the equipment, Gloria and I will layout the attack plans for the Penthouse and the Lenora! Let's be prepared to move on the Penthouse at 0130 hour!

Chapter 28

A close call . . . .

On the way to the Seattle Airport, fog and a lite mist began to shroud the airport.

With fog lights shining and the misty rain falling, it left Marie with somewhat of an eerie feeling. She remembered it was this type weather the night she lost her dear friend, FBI Agent, Steve Hightower, while assisting the Treasury Department on a raid gone bad.

A lot of changes had occurred in her life since then. Her work with Dave Snider and Jack Abbott had kept her busy and left her very little time to think about the past.

Suddenly silence was broken when a Seattle Police unit passed with red lights flashing and the siren blasting.

Doug asked, "Okay young lady you've got something on your mind. What's going on?"

"Oh, you noticed! I was thinking back on the night we were involved with the Treasury Department. I know you miss Steve too. He thought a lot of you and was always pleased with your assistance. I was thinking about the weather being the same as tonight."

Reaching across the seat, Doug placed his right hand on Marie's left shoulder, "Pretty Lady, you've got to quit blaming yourself for his loss. Tonight, let's think about staying alive to finish this assignment."

As they drove up the parking garage ramp, a local airport security vehicle was parked along side Marie's Ford. The security officer was outside his vehicle with flash light in hand while checking the Vehicle Identification Number; also from time to time, he would flash the light inside the Ford.

With a firm voice Marie said, "Doug, you are my lover. You've just picked me up on my arrival from Chicago. Since the vehicle is showing an Illinois license tag we'll be okay. I'll pretend I'm out here for the Regatta but had to return to Chicago for a friend's funeral. Let's pray to God that he buys my story. Don't be alarmed, I moving over close to you. You may refer to me as 'Darling' and a hug now and then will be okay. Are you ready?"

Doug replied with a grin, "Darling, all systems are on go!"

The security officer was a mature male and seemed to be concerned about the vehicle in question. He made an effort to check underneath Marie's vehicle. Doug stopped the Avis Rental Car approximately fifteen feet from the officer. Both he and Marie stepped out of the vehicle and greeted him.

"Good evening officer. Is there a problem?"

"Yes, you are parked in a restricted zone. Vehicles left in this area over eighteen hours are subject to being towed! Do one of you own this vehicle?"

"Yes Sir. The automobile belongs to me," Marie immediately replied.

Doug said, "Darling, it's okay. Show the officer your I.D. and vehicle registration. Doug pulled Marie close and hugged and kissed her as to have the hug serve as a calming effort.

The officer found Marie's papers were in order; then he turned his attention to Doug.

"And who are you?"

"My name is Doug Taylor and I'm here for the Regatta." Looking at Marie, darling, we're going to be late if we're to meet Jack and Gloria at the Baker Hotel! "Doug's statement was an attempt to divert the officer's attention from Marie's vehicle."

The security officer looking at the couple commented, "Well, you may be a little bit late. I have a wrecker on the way to tow this unit to safe storage!"

Doug pleaded, "Officer my Lady has had a tough day with the funeral in Chicago and now you are wanting to tow her car away. How about me paying the tow charge and let's call it a day?"

Looking directly toward Doug, "Mister are you trying to bribe me?"

Doug realized he must move fast. "No Sir, I'm just trying to be reasonable. I would need a receipt."

Marie acted on impulse. She put her arms around Doug's neck and said. "I love you and I've missed you."

The security officer was somewhat amused and said, "Get the hell off this airport or I'm going to give you both a ticket for disturbing the peace!"

The next stop for the impostors would be the Starlight Motel. Doug had certainly enjoyed the little escapade at the Seattle Airport and the truth be known, he would like to enjoy a repeat performance if Marie felt up to it. They checked into the motel as husband and wife and love making was the last thing Marie would be considering. Her job was to select the weaponry best suited for the schedule assault on the Penthouse. It took forty five minutes to make the weapon selections and load the equipment into the Avis Rent Car.

At this point, the Wolf and Gloria had mapped out the assault plans which included nullifying the power boat activities. If they were successful in eliminating the power boats, then the Cartel's force would be divided. This in turn would leave a small group aboard the Lenora.

When Marie and Doug drove into the Baker parking garage they noticed some of Seattle's police officers were milling around the garage entrance. At this point they had to proceed with caution because of the weapons they had in their possession. They were thankful they had taken time at the motel to load the weapons into the Avis Rent-a-Car. For a moment they could rest easy because now the weapons had been moved to the place of the attack.

When they arrived, the Wolf greeted them warmly and seemed to be very pleased upon their return. "Glad you made it back. By the way Doug, you may want to straighten your lipstick."

"I can explain." Marie said.

"Absolutely no need to explain. We've got work to do; after the work, we can have fun and games. Let me go over the plan of attack!"

Marie declared, "But it's not what you think!"

"One more time Marie . . . forget it, we've got a lot of work to do and our lives are on the line. No more conversation, understood?"

With tears in her eyes Marie responded, yes sir."

Again the first part of the attack was reviewed, since the power boats were so important to the Cartel's operation. The Wolf felt it extremely important not to mess up in the beginning, because so much of their attack plan depended on exact timing.

He laid out the initial plan. "Marie, at 0100 hours you and Doug take care of the guards on the power boats, then tamper with the wiring to make the boats non-operative.

It's likely the other Cartel members will be partying until 0300 to 0400 hours in the Penthouse area. By approximately 0120 hours, you should be able to accomplish your mission! He continued . . . .

"At 0110 Gloria will manage to be invited to the Penthouse. We've decided she will be working the hotel bar. We feel she can accomplish the fete by her alluring looks at some of the Cartel members frequenting the bar. If for some reason the 'come on' doesn't work, then she will move to the Penthouse area and 'work' the guard on duty."

"Doug asked the Wolf, "What will you be doing while all this is going on?"

"I'll be utilizing the freight elevators to move the needed equipment to the sixteenth floor. When I checked out the hotel floor plan, I noticed a huge utility closet near the elevator shaft. This area is extremely important logistically if our mission is to succeed here at the hotel. At exactly 0127 hours, I plan to set off two smoke grenades, one in the stairwell, the other in the passenger service elevators. Immediately thereafter, we should all be in place on the sixteenth floor to assault the Penthouse.

"I wish I could tell you this operation was not needed; however, to stop the Cartels I have deemed the action necessary if our world is to be made a better place to live."

A frown came across Doug's face. "What about the collateral damage? I'm concerned a lot of innocent bystanders are going to be killed or injured."

"Doug, I realize your combat experience is very limited. I want you to know it hurts me personally to see the innocent suffer; but we must realize, we are in a war which sets no boundaries or rules of engagement. Again, the element of surprise is important to help reduce the collateral damage.

"This morning I want you to think only about the children who suffer at the hands of these bastards. When I think about it my blood runs cold!

"It is essential we get out of this hotel immediately after the Penthouse attack. I have scheduled the helicopter to take two of us directly to Sequim. Doug and Marie will travel by car to Sequim to bring the assault weapons, and the diving equipment. When you leave your hotel rooms make sure you have all your gear. A trace of your presence is not to be left. Does everyone understand? We must realize all of Seattle will be 'up in arms' about this attack. I have set our attack on the Lenora at 0700 hours.

"I'm hoping the Lenora's Captain will be in the Penthouse area. If so, the sailing of the Lenora will be delayed for several hours. It is extremely important we catch the Lenora while she is still anchored in the "Strait.""

Chapter 29

Old friends meet again!

Detective Ed Simpson and Chris Salazar were sharing drinks at the Baker Hotel Street Cafe, when Frank Cortez and the beautiful Loretta approached their table. Cortez asked, "Senor, Salazar may we join you?"

Smiling, Salazar said, "Absolutely! Please meet my friend, Ed Simpson. Simpson is a detective out of Chicago. We sometimes work together." A quick glance at Loretta told Simpson he was at the right place at the right time!

With his eyebrows arched, Cortez asked, "Detective what brings you to Seattle?"

"I'm here to enjoy the Regatta."

"Si, it should be a great race." Cortez commented.

The waitress arrived and Cortez ordered another round of drinks for his friends.

Suddenly, Salazar spotted Marie Higgins approaching the cafe. He asked the group to excuse him for a moment and he headed for Marie. At this point Doug Taylor was trailing Marie and viewed the action. He watched as Salazar hugged Marie and took her arm as he escorted her over to Cortez and his group. Salazar was smiling as he introduced Marie to the entire group and seated her next to Cortez.

Doug Taylor located a table near the group in hopes he could overhear their conversation.

After Salazar had ordered Marie a drink, one of the sailors from the power boat appeared along side Cortez. A conservation ensued, however it was in Spanish and Doug could not understand.

As Marie took a sip of her drink, she motioned to Doug not to interfere. Cortez stood up and gave a toast in Spanish and the group laughed. He then made a quick announcement, the group was heading for the Lenora! As the group stood up a look of concern came across Marie Higgins face. She was not in control!

Rapidly sizing up the situation, Doug decided to move in on the group and pose as Marie's drunken lover. Maybe he could change the course of action.

Doug yelled in slurred speech, "Marie, darling, I thought we were suppose to meet in the hotel bar."

Cortez pulled a .8mm Lugger and shoved it against Doug's rib cage. "Senor, back off!"

Salazar stepped in between the two men and said. "Cortez, that will not be necessary. The man has had too much to drink. Let me handle this! Cortez re-holstered his piece.

Salazar smiling, "Fellow, I do not know who you are but Marie is with me. I suggest you move on and sober up. Cortez will kill you, move!"

Both Marie and Doug realized the whole operation was at stake if they made the wrong moves. Marie would be forced to go in the power boat to the Lenora.

Doug took Salazar's advice and backed off, slowly moving down near the dock area. He watched helplessly as the Cortez party boarded the number one power boat. As the sailor put the boat in reverse, Marie gave Doug a 'thumbs-up' sign as to assure him she could and would handle the situation. As the power boat sped out of sight in Puget Sound waters, Doug called the Wolf.

"He answered his cell phone. "Yes."

"We've got a serious problem, Marie has been escorted to one of the power boats and they are on their way to the Lenora!"

"What the hell are you talking about?" He yelled into his cell phone.

Doug responded, "I'm at the docks, hurry down and I will explain in detail!"

Within five minutes, both the Wolf and Gloria were standing beside Doug on the pier next to the power boat docking area.

With a firm voice he asked, "Doug, why didn't you stop her?"

"Let me give you the setting. We had decided to operate separately. She's was walking several feet in front of me when she encountered Chris Salazar. I think it was Salazar. He took her by the arm and pulled her toward their table. Immediately, one of the drug king-pins of the Cartel showed up with a good-looking woman on his arm, and they joined the group. Apparently, this Salazar was well acquainted with the man. The next thing Marie realized, she was caught in the middle because of her acquaintance with Salazar.

"Within five minutes the whole situation developed and was out of our control. I posed as a drunken lover in an attempt to have Marie come with me, but the cartel guy placed the barrel of a 8 mm Lugger against my rib cage. This Salazar fellow probably saved my life! As the power boat sped away, Marie gave me a 'thumbs-up' as though she could handle the situation."

With a scowl on his face, the Wolf showed anger. "Damn, you did the best you could, we've got to speed up our attack! I guess the other power boat is near the Lenora. Doug you can assist me in moving the equipment up to the sixteenth floor. Gloria, we'll meet you in the Penthouse. I have every confidence you'll be able to gain entrance."

With a faint smile Gloria said, "After I change into something more comfortable and clear my room, I'll see what I can do with the boys from the Lenora. You guys be careful!"

The Wolf secured a clothes moving cart from the hotel check-in-area and loaded a part of his hanging wardrobe on the clothes rack. From all appearances it looked as though he was checking into the hotel. As he and Doug were loading the cart with assault equipment, a hotel security unit drove slowly pass. The security guard waved and yelled, "Welcome aboard! You folks enjoy the Regatta." He and Doug, had again 'dodged another bullet'. The security guard thought they were new arrivals for the Regatta week-end.

Smiling, the Wolf said, "We're lucky bastards. The hanging clothes and cart did the trick."

Chapter 30

The Wolf's reconnaissance paid off, as the large sixteenth floor utility closet made an excellent storage facility for the assault equipment. The entry was made without incident and the two men could clearly hear all the festivities going on in the Penthouse. Within a few minutes, the elevator doors opened and Gloria was walking arm in arm with two drunken sailors.

When the guard opened the door to the Penthouse parlor, Gloria glanced back toward the utility closet as to say, 'I'm on schedule.'

Doug commented, "Damn, Gloria is some good-looking!"

In a very low voice, the Wolf replied, "Yeah I know, try to keep your mind on business."

Both the men had slipped on white coveralls and caps found in the utility room, and now would appear to be hotel utility workers. The coveralls afforded ample room for both men to conceal short double-barrel.12 gauge shotguns, plus their 9mm Glock handguns and two fragmented grenades. At exactly 0127 hours, the Wolf dropped the first smoke bomb in the open elevator on the sixteenth floor. Then with cat like moves, he ran to the stairway located near the elevator shaft and dropped the second smoke bomb. Within a short time, the fire alarms would sound and the Brown Hotel would be put on alert. If they were to benefit from the element of surprise, they must move rapidly to assault the cartel members in the Penthouse Suite.

Doug had engaged the guard at the Penthouse entrance in conversation contending, he needed to check the air conditioning unit. The guard seemed to be totally confused as he did not understand why the unit needed to be checked during the early morning hour. Suddenly, the Wolf appeared and Doug introduced him as his supervisor. He did not utter a word as he pushed a six inch stiletto knife blade into the guard's chest just left of his sternum! The guard let out a small groan and fell to the floor, dead.

Doug looking alarmed, "Damn, you don't mess around do you?"

The reply was brief, "I don't have time."

When they entered the Penthouse parlor area, the party was in full swing and very few even noticed the two men dressed as hotel utility workers. First things first, they had to locate Gloria. The Wolf noticed all the Penthouse bedrooms were being used by the occupants to have sex or for the partaking of drugs, not necessarily in any particular order! A quick check of each bedroom did not produce the whereabouts of Gloria.

As Doug entered the dining area, he found Gloria backed up against the dining table with Juan Corzion attempting to fondle her. One of the sailors was holding Gloria's right arm behind her back, as Corsion unbuttoned her blouse and was positioning himself to work on her breast. Gloria seeing Doug knew they had been successful in making entry into the Penthouse and the element of surprise was most beneficial. It was time for her to make her move!

She let out a blood curdling screen while kicking Corzion in the groin. She whirled to face the sailor and planted her left foot on his right knee and crushed the knee joint. By this time Corzion was upright. She pulled a .22 Colt automatic from her waistband and placed the barrel under his right jaw bone and pulled the trigger. The .22 long hollow point shell blew a large hole in Corizon's skull. His fondling and drug dealing days had come to a sudden end!

In the Penthouse lounging area, the Wolf had encountered the three Thailand recruiters, along with the Zeta Cartel members and three homosexuals openly engaged in a sexual frenzy.

He fired four rounds from his 12 gauge shotgun. In eighteen seconds twelve people lay dead in the lounging area. He laid a silver wolf signet on the coffee table. With Doug killing two cartel members in the kitchen area, a total of fifteen bad hombres had been eliminated. The surprise element has always been essential in combat and on this occasion it kept the collateral damage at a minimum and prevented return fire from the AK47's! However, three good-looking prostitutes were killed in the assault. Looking at it on a realistic basis, one would have to say, they were at the wrong place at the wrong time.

Doug with a very serious look on his face said, "I think we have another problem. One of the sailors I shot in the kitchen area was talking on the phone to someone on the Lenora."

The Wolf, Gloria, and Doug heard the sirens in the distance and knew it was time to exit the building via the service elevator to the parking garage. Within thirty-minutes, he and Gloria would be at the heliport and Doug would be driving toward Pillar Point. Big Target, the Lenora!

At the heliport while awaiting for the chopper to be serviced, Gloria became inquisitive.

"Jack, tell me, what do you do with your spare time? Do you have someone special in your life?"

For the first time in a long while, Jack Abbott was speechless. The inquiry took him by total surprise. Finally his thought processing came back and he asked himself the number one question. Why would this good-looking creature ask me this question?' Gaining his composure he smiled, and paused.

"Well, . . . for the last few years, I haven't had a lot of spare time which leads me to the second part of your inquiry. Not having time to devote to establishing a meaningful relationship, I did not attempt to do so, until now!"

Gloria pushing her long hair back, while looking into Jack's eyes, said. "Mister, you don't waste any time do you?"

"No Mam, not since you are involved!"

Gently he reached over, placing both hands on her shoulders and pulled her close. He placed his right hand on her bottom lip and parted it, while gently kissing her. As he started to pull back,Gloria opened her mouth wider and held the kiss. As their lips parted she said.

"It's been a long, long time!"

Chapter 31

The Lenora . . . 0200 Hours.

Frank Cortez, leader of the Villarrell cartel and Arthur Valdez, leader of the Sinaloa cartel were standing on the bridge of the Lenora watching the power boats maneuver along side the ship. A sailor approached Cortez and informed him, communications had been lost with the cartel group in Seattle. Cortez immediately called for all ship personnel to report to the stateroom.

Salazar knew he must keep a close watch on Marie Higgins, aka., Helen Schroeder as she had caught the roaming eye of Cortez. He knew Cortez like the back of his hand. If given the opportunity to take, Marie he would do so, even if it resulted in an act of rape. Both Salazar and Marie had heard the boatswain's whistle to assemble the crew. Salazar felt he must leave Marie in her cabin while he checked out the commotion.

"Marie, I want you to stay in your cabin. Do not open the door for anyone. We have some rough hombres aboard this ship and they enjoy white women. I'll be back shortly."

"What if Mr. Cortez comes calling?"

"Anyone, includes him. I had him in mind when I gave you the instruction. Cortez is a very dangerous man. I want to try to avoid confrontation with him if at all possible!"

"Chris, one question before you go. Are you on his payroll?"

Chris Salazar smiling said, "as needed". With the curt remark, he slammed the cabin door and headed for the stateroom to meet with Cortez.

Occasionally puffing on a Cuban cigar, Cortez, was pacing back and forth in front of his assembled seaman and some guest. He had a hard time keeping the important subject matter on his mind, since some of the guest were scantly dressed, with open blouses and skirts pulled up above their knees. Salazar arrived just as Cortez began his speech.

"We have a big problem. We have lost communications with our associates in Seattle.

It is possible they are under attack or have been arrested on drug charges; or whatever, I want the machine guns activated immediately. We will pull anchor at 0800 hours with or without our friends in Seattle.

"Salazar, I see you have joined our meeting. Since some of the law enforcement amigos may be headed this way, I want you to join my associate, Arthur Valdez on the bridge watch. We've got five to six hours before we set sail. If the Amigos come I want you to welcome them aboard, understood?"

"Mr. Cortez, I understand but I have a special guest aboard. I need to be with her."

Smiling, Cortez replied. "My dear friend, I will see after her and I will bring her to you before dawn."

For the first time Salazar's dealings with Frank Cortez had gone sour. A lump came in his throat and he began to sweat. He knew exactly what Cortez had in mind. He also knew the time element was extremely important. Approximately five to six hours made a big difference. First, he knew Marie was not in immediate danger because she had her cabin door secured; yet, he knew Cortez would be able in time to enter the cabin. If Marie continued to deny him entry, sooner or later, he would have his executive officer furnish him a key.

Secondly, in some way he had to figure out a way to handle Arthur Valdez while working with him on the bridge. Likewise, he must get Simpson involved in helping Marie. The problems with Simpson's involvement was twofold. It seemed he was preoccupied with the beautiful, Loretta and he did not fully understand how ruthless Cortez could be. No doubt about it, Simpson was impressed with Cortez and his evidenced wealth. He had nothing on his mind other than making out with Loretta.

As Salazar headed for the bridge to start his tour of duty with Valdez, Simpson and Loretta were entering her cabin. It was an opportune time for Salazar to approach Simpson.

"Hey, mate how's it going?"

Simpson replied, "Man it doesn't get any better than this!"

Salazar making direct eye contact with Simpson, "In a couple of hours, come up to the bridge, I need to visit with you, okay?"

Grinning, Simpson answered, "You bet, if I have enough strength left to climb those twelve steps to the bridge."

Frowning, Salazar replied, "You'd better save your energy, it may mean life or death!"

By this time, Loretta was hot to trot and she grabbed Simpson by his left arm and pulled him inside her cabin. Salazar climbed to the bridge area where Arthur Valdez was waiting.

He was totally surprised to find Valdez, a black man and was impressed with his mannerisms.

"Welcome aboard, senor. Are you a sailor?" Valdez asked."

"Only small lake craft," Salazar replied.

"Good, the same principles apply. I understand you are with the FBI. Is this correct?"

"Yes, however I do special work for Frank Cortez."

"That is good. Mr. Cortez and I have been friends and business associates for many years. I could tell by the expression on your face, you were surprised to find me a black man. It's a long story. My dad was from South Africa and I was brought up being involved in the slave trade business. That's were I learned sailing."

Looking very serious, Salazar said, "I hope we don't set sail before our people return from Seattle. I have close friends who went ashore. Have you heard any reports from that group?"

"No, our communications were cut off abruptly. I think I heard gun fire prior to being dis-connected. Please excuse me, I must check with our crew on the .50 caliber guns located on the bow and stern. I'll be back in about fifteen minutes. Do you need anything before I go?"

Salazar responded, "No, I'll be okay. I'll keep a close watch; however, it seems visibility is limited since the fog is getting heavier."

Chapter 32

Doug was making good time on Highway 112 on his route to Sequim. As the moon shed light, he could tell the fog was becoming heavier and as a result he had to curtail his speed.

Approximately twelve miles east of Sequim, he began to feel a bumping of his left front tire and suddenly the tire blew. He managed to control the vehicle and pull off on the right shoulder of the road. This automatically presented a major problem. With the weaponry he had packed in the trunk of the car, he had to move some of it to the floor board of the back seat area to be able to reach the spare tire and wheel.

He had been thoughtful enough to set out reflectors before jacking the vehicle up to change the tire. He thought to himself how fortunate there's very little traffic on Highway 112 during this early morning hour. Suddenly, a vehicle rounded a curve and immediately turned on overhead lights, shinning red, white, and blue, a Washington Highway Patrol vehicle approached!

The patrol officer was, Corporal Angie Walker. As she stepped out of the patrol vehicle, she left the headlamps of the patrol unit shinning on Doug, as he mounted the spare tire and wheel on his vehicle.

"Good morning, you picked a terrible time to have a blow-out," she said with a smile.

"Yeah, I'm not very good at this type thing," Doug answered.

Walker inquired, "What brings you out at this early morning hour?"

"I'm meeting friends at Sequim for a little scuba diving this morning."

"May I see your driver's license," officer Walker asked.

As Doug was fumbling for his driver's license, Walker walked around the vehicle, moving her flashlight up and down while peering in the front and back seats. Finally Doug found his fake driver's license and handed them to Walker.

"Oh, I see you are from Chicago. You are a long way from home Mr. Taylor. What type of work do you do?"

"Well, I'm somewhat a 'Jack of All Trades'. I'm representing the lumber industry at the present time; however I took a few days off to enjoy the Regatta and do some scuba diving."

"Yeah, I noticed the fine looking scuba gear you've piled in the back seat area. Listen, I've got to move on. Good luck and be careful on this narrow highway," Officer Walker waved as she pulled her patrol car past his vehicle.

Dave Snider, aka, Doug Taylor was not a religious man, but he knelt down and thanked God for his mercy. If he had not been able to satisfy officer Walker during her inquiry, it would have been necessary to eliminate her or the assignment would fail. He felt like a nervous wreck but he must move on to meet the helicopter in Sequim.

Both Jack Abbott and Gloria Hampton boarded the helicopter feeling they had finally found someone to love. By this time, the helicopter pilot had been around Jack enough he could tell he had a different demeanor . . . . he was smiling! Looking over he saw Jack put his arm around Gloria and pull her close. Since he had seen Gloria only once before he could not tell if she was a new acquaintance, but he certainly could tell there existed a mutual admiration society between the two of them.

The Wolf begin to consider the danger both were facing. It did not give him a warm and fuzzy feeling knowing Gloria would soon be involved in combat. He looked over at Gloria and whispered.

"Pretty lady, I'm thinking you should stay at Pillar Point and serve as backup, while Doug and I finish this assignment."

Smiling, Gloria responded, "Now there you go wanting to be a protector. You'll have to remember, I'm the only one at this party who's had Naval Seal training! I'll be the one who places the explosive charges on the keel of the Lenora."

"Colonel, sounds like you are already pulling rank on me."

"Darling, you are absolutely correct!"

"Well Colonel let me remind you, this is my assignment and you were ordered to assist me. If I want you to stay ashore . . . you'll stay ashore!" The helicopter pilot laughed out loud. With a scowl on her face, Gloria looked directly at the pilot.

The pilot immediately apologized, "I'm sorry I didn't mean to intervene. We all recognize somebody has to be in charge. I'll go along with Jack on this one."

For the first time, Gloria displayed her temperament and addressed the helicopter pilot.

"Sir, I respect your position and your ability to fly this aircraft, but you've started meddling into an area which is absolutely none of your business. I will not stay behind while Jack and Doug go into harms way. We have a lady aboard the Lenora who needs my help."

Now, the Wolf recognized why she wore the rank of Colonel. Both he and the Pilot decided to talk about the weather conditions. He observed a lone vehicle traveling northwest on Highway 112 and he hoped it was Doug bringing the necessary equipment to make war!

He pulled Gloria over close and gently kissed her, as he said. "My beautiful Gloria, I want you to know I'm extremely proud of you."

Doug drove the Avis vehicle onto the helicopter parking lot. He glanced up and saw the helicopter flashing lights as it was approaching the landing area. He in turn repeatedly turned his vehicle lights on and off to signal his arrival.

The Wolf instructed the helicopter pilot to begin circling the Lenora promptly at 0500 hours and continue at thirty minute intervals. The pilot agreed as long as dark prevailed and the fog was thick. He remembered the.50 Caliber machine guns on the bow and stern of the Lenora.

The drive from Sequim to Pillar Point was spent in reviewing the map of Pillar Point, in particular the beach structure as related to the location of the Lenora. She lay anchored approximately two to three hundred feet off shore. The water depth was twenty-five to forty feet at anchor point. The scuba gear was top of its class, along with the spear guns and support equipment. All systems were on go! The only difficulty at this point was the abundance of harbor seals. To the experienced diver it was not a major problem. However, a diver should make a mental note, 'where there's harbor seals', sometimes sharks are close by. With it being early morning hour, it could be time for a shark's morning breakfast. The watchword among the assault team was for each member to stay alert!

At 0440 hours they would arrived at Pillar Point cove to launch their rubber boat.

It was time to synchronize their watches since timing was extremely important. If all goes well, the 'Chopper' would be over the Lenora at 0500 hours, this in turn would assist in diverting attention of the crew members aboard ship. The Wolf would board the Lenora's bow, Doug would board her at the stern, while Gloria would go underwater to place three C-4 explosive charges on the keel, near the bow, mid-ship, and stern.

Chapter 33

0455 hours aboard the Lenora . . . . Things were heating up!

Simpson was a very frustrated man. Loretta had done her job for Cortez! She had played the part of temptress to gain information from Simpson. Actually, she was to find out if Simpson was associated in business with Salazar. Loretta was Cortez's woman and she was not about to have sex with Simpson or anyone else at this point. In truth, she was terrified of Cortez as she had seen way too many killings! Simpson had given up in his conquest to seduce Loretta and had dozed off on her bed.

Suddenly his cell phone rang, it was Captain Turner in Chicago! The ring of the phone had startled Simpson but he was awake enough to take the call.

In a very low voice, he said, "Hello".

Captain Turner was chewing on his old stogie. "Simpson, I know it's an early hour in your neck of the woods but I need to know what the hell's going on. Bring your Captain up to date!" Loretta was standing at bedside to listen to every word Simpson said in reply.

"Chief, everything is going as planned. Salazar and I are going to the Regatta today and we're both on top of this case."

"What do you mean you're both on top of this case? Have you got a couple of 'broads' in your hotel room?"

Simpson responded rapidly. "No sir, nothing like that!"

Chief Turner was restless. "What's this I hear about three Latino's being murdered at the Brown hotel? Best I recall that's where you are staying."

"Yes sir, I was going to put that in my written report. Salazar is involved in the investigation. He's keeping me informed as best he can."

Chief Turner asked a very pertinent question, "Simpson where are you located now?"

"I'm aboard a Spanish sailing vessel, the Lenora," Simpson replied.

"You're where?"

With a very low voice, Simpson said it again. "I'm aboard a Spanish sailing vessel, the Lenora."

"Simpson, you're drunk, aren't you?"

"No sir, I can explain later. I'll give you a call back in a couple of hours." The phone line went open.

Actually, Simpson was glad he received the surprise phone call, because it helped him to realize he had been set-up. He had to find Salazar. He pushed Loretta down on the bed and headed for the ship's bridge. As he passed Marie's cabin, Frank Cortez was descending the stairway from the second deck.

Cortez was smiling, "Senor Simpson, are you enjoying your stay aboard the Lenora?"

Seeming to be cheerful, Simpson replied, "Thanks to you, I'm having the time of my life."

"Oh, you finding Loretta a good woman for you, yes?"

Now Simpson was in a state of quandary in how to answer Cortez's question. If he indicated he had sex with Loretta she would be in deep trouble, on the other hand he should in some way show satisfaction with being in Loretta's company. He made his reply simple.

"Mr. Cortez, Loretta is a very nice lady. She talked to me about Spain and told me how beautiful it is, I hope someday to visit your country."

"Did you have this woman, Loretta?"

"No, we just talked."

Cortez did not give up his questioning about Loretta. "No sex with this, Loretta?"

Simpson looked directly into Cortez's eyes, "None."

At this point Simpson felt he had graded Cortez correctly, and possibly saved Loretta from abuse. Then Cortez changed his line of questioning to inquire about Salazar and Simpson's business relationship.

"Tell me Senor, you and Salazar work as partners, yes?"

Smiling, Simpson answered, "Sometimes we do."

With his eyebrows arched, Cortez declared, "This Salazar, FBI man, he make a lot of money!"

"Yes, I know," Simpson confirmed.

As Cortez and Simpson conversation continued Cortez had reached his destination, Marie's cabin! Simpson excused himself by saying, "Mr. Cortez have a good morning," He continued on his way to the bridge to find Salazar. Simpson's mission had become urgent when he realized Cortez was in pursuit of Marie.

As Cortez knocked on Marie's cabin door he could hear her talking on her cell phone.

"Marie, this is Frank Cortez, I need to see you."

There was no immediate response. Again, he knocked on the cabin door and repeated himself. Now there was silence as he could not hear Marie talking to anyone. Her first call had been to the Wolf, then she realized his cell phone had been turned off, same with Doug and Gloria. It was easy for her to understand why their assault team was operating in a silent mode.

She had just left word on Salazar's cell phone to call her, that's when she heard Cortez at the door.

"Yes, Mr. Cortez, what do you need at this hour?"

"You!"

"I understand, but I'm not an early morning person, and besides I'm ill."

"Senorita, that's okay, I am also a doctor. Open the cabin door!"

With a loud voice, Marie replied. "It's best you go away. I will see you at breakfast."

"Senorita, you open door. I will find a key to your cabin door and I will come back."

Simpson found Salazar on the ship's bridge having coffee with Valdez. It was important he stay calm as he approached Salazar. He certainly did not know Valdez or his temperament.

With a sleepy sounding voice, Simpson said, "Good morning, this early hour. I couldn't sleep and I smelled fresh coffee brewing, mind if I join you?"

Valdez answered, "Si Senor, help yourself."

Salazar stepped forward. "Valdez, meet my business associate, Ed Simpson. We're both from the Chicago area and have worked together for some time."

Smiling, Valdez extended his right hand to greet Simpson, "Good to have you aboard, Senor Simpson. Please help yourself to mucho coffee, I must use the 'head'. I'll be back one momento."

Simpson was in luck, because Valdez's absence gave him the opportunity to discuss Marie and Cortez. He set his coffee cup down near the ship's compass. Reaching out he put his hand on Salazar's shoulder and pulled him up close.

In a whispering tone Simpson said, "We've got a big problem. Cortez is trying to gain entrance to Marie's cabin. Do you want me to take him out or do you want to handle it in some other way?"

"I'll handle Cortez, Marie is my responsibility! Tell Valdez I had to go to my cabin and I will be back shortly."

Chapter 34

The Assault!

The Pillar Point cove was covered in heavy fog as the trio launched the rubber boat on the seventh wave. The pilot of the yacht had shown good judgment by anchoring the Lenora in the calm cove waters. Each member of the assault team realized they must employ a soft and smooth rowing technique to reduce the noise at water level. Within twenty feet of the Lenora, they pulled their oars and drifted up to her bow.

The Wolf quietly tied the boat to the ship anchor line, as Gloria slipped into the water and dove to the ship's keel level. Her visibility was good as the yacht's security lights reflected in the water. On occasion a harbor seal would swim by and give her an inquisitive look as she was strapping a charge to the keel. She had previously set the explosive charges to detonate at 0700 hours. Suddenly she heard movement up topside of the Lenora. She determined it was the crews reaction to the helicopter's noise overhead. She was on time, and doing her job without interference.

As the Wolf pulled himself up the anchor chain line, Doug slipped over the side of the rubber boat, and swam quietly to the stern section to neutralize the guard, plus the .50 caliber machine gun position. He had never used a Gulf Magnum Spear Gun before; however, he knew that sometimes divers used the weapon against sharks, so he felt he should have no problem using it against a seaman.

Up at the bow, when the Wolf peered over the guard rail he saw the seaman had left the .50 caliber machine gun unguarded and was taking a stretch brake while lighting a cigarette. The Wolf moved to the gun in-placement, as he pulled his stiletto knife from his leg holster. The seaman heard the noise and turned to face his attacker. He was too slow in re-acting, as the Wolf pushed the blade into his rib cage, penetrating his heart. The seaman only let out a muffled sound and died instantly. The Wolf moved to the machine gun and removed the belt of ammunition and threw it overboard; then he placed a small incendiary bomb in the guns firing chamber near the bolt area and set the timer for explosion at 0630 hours.

At the stern, Doug took three small ball bearings out of his equipment sack and threw one against the port side of the ship as he tread water. The spear gun had a thirty foot range so it was important he stay within ten foot of the Lenora. The first ball bearing did not attract the seaman; however, the second one did. As the seaman peered over the bow of the ship, he made a good target. Doug did not hesitate, as he aimed the spear-gun at chest level and fired. The seaman did not make a sound as Doug pulled him by the spear gun line into the water. The seaman was dead.

Gloria surfaced near the stern as she had completed placing three C-4 charges on the hull of the Lenora. Now time was of the essence, it would not be long before daylight and the ships company would be moving about and soon discover the attack was underway. There were several people the trio needed to locate. First was

Marie, then Salazar, and Simpson. The Wolf, Gloria and Doug met in a hatchway mid-ship and would move out according to their pre-assigned areas of responsibility.

The helicopter again passed over the Lenora and made three circles at a very low altitude, as the sun was beginning to break through the fog.

Marie's cabin was becoming a busy place. Cortez had made an un-invited entry into her cabin. It seemed his hormones had kicked in, and he had to have a woman at early hour. Marie was found without weapon as she had placed her Glock hand-gun in the overhead bin. She would attempt to talk her way out of a very difficult situation.

Cortez had managed to press her against the bulkhead and was kissing her on the neck.

Somewhat frantic, Marie said, "Senor Cortez, I explained to you I'm ill. I was trying to tell you it is very uncomfortable for me to have sex this time of month!"

"Senorita, it makes no difference to me. You are beautiful and it will not take me long."

Salazar knocked on Marie's cabin door. "Marie, may I come in?"

In a calm voice she said, "No."

In a loud voice, Salazar said. "I must see you immediately!"

Marie trying to save Salazar's life, said, "Please go away."

Up on the bridge the fog had lifted, Valdez saw the body of the dead seaman laying on deck near the .50 caliber machine gun. He sounded the ship alarm system for all seaman to report to their battle stations! Now the war was on and the Wolf was ready for battle. He opened fire on two seaman coming up the stairwell to the top deck. Another seaman ran for the .50 caliber machine gun located on the bow. As he reached the piece, the incendiary bomb exploded catching him on fire. It was not a pretty sight as he dove into the chilling water.

Simpson's law enforcement experience told him a war was on. Being one of the good guys, he attacked Valdez by shoving his head through one of the bridge starboard windows. The glass breakage caused severe bleeding around Valdez's eyes and forehead. Valdez retaliated by kicking Simpson in the groin. Realizing he was in mortal danger, Simpson grabbed the fire-ax hanging on the bulkhead and swung it from right to left striking Valdez above the left ear. The battle was over almost as fast as it had started. Valdez lay dead at Simpson's feet!

Salazar knew Marie would never respond to him by asking him to go away. Marie was in trouble! He immediately backed up and ran toward the cabin door ramming it open with his right shoulder.

The cabin door burst open and Salazar rushed toward Cortez. Cortez did not hesitate as he threw a large hunting knife which sank into Salazar's chest. Salazar sank to his knees gasping for air as blood streamed from his mouth. Quickly Marie ran to his aid, Cortez ran passed her and headed for the ship's bridge. As he exited the hatchway he encountered the Wolf face to face!

At first Cortez seemed startled; yet he realized his ship was under attack. The Wolf could tell by the way Cortez was dressed, he was an important man, maybe he had lucked out.

Cortez spoke first. "Hombre, who are you and what are you doing aboard my ship?"

With a slight smile, I'm the Wolf and I'm here to sink this ship!"

"I'm Senor Cortez and I am in charge of this vessel. Get off the Lenora."

"Cortez, the Lenora is going down and you're going with her! He pitched a silver wolf signet toward Cortez.

"Senor, you are a very ignorant man. Do you think I will allow you to do this?"

"Senor Cortez. your chances of stopping me are slim to none."

Suddenly, both men could hear the fire-fight taking place down below. It seems Gloria and Doug had encountered three seamen equipped with AK 47's! The fire-fight didn't last long, when Gloria tossed two grenades. The explosion tore part of the upper deck apart. Simpson was caught up in the explosion and was blow overboard. He was in frigid water and swam toward the bow of the ship. He realized he needed help, as parts of his body were becoming numb.

Frank Cortez now realized the Wolf was not a solo act. He made a mad rush toward him; the Wolf dropped to the deck in a spinning motion and placed his left leg in front of Cortez's right ankle bringing him down. He immediately was on top of Cortez. Without uttering another word, the Wolf cupped his left hand and placed it under Cortez's chin, then placed his right hand on the back of Cortez's head, while giving it a quick twist. Instantly, he heard the snapping sound of Cortez's spine. Cortez's days of fun and games had come to a sudden end!

Suddenly, they heard the retracting of the ship's anchor chain . . . . the ship engines were started. The Wolf was the first to make a move toward the bridge, followed by Doug. Gloria headed toward Marie's cabin. When the Wolf entered the bridge area he encountered a wounded seaman at the helm of the ship. The man had been caught in the grenade attack and was bleeding badly. He looked directly at the Wolf and collapsed. The Wolf tried to administer to his wounds but he was dead. Doug reached over the helm and put the engines in neutral and the two headed for Gloria and Marie. The Wolf looking at his watch knew they had five minutes to clear the Lenora as she was about to explode.

When Gloria reached Marie she was holding Salazar in her arms and was crying. Gloria gently reached down and put her arms around Marie and said, "Marie, I understand. You were still in love with him weren't you?"

With tears flowing down her cheeks, Marie replied. "Yes, but I didn't realize it!"

The Wolf and Doug were standing at the cabin door listening as Gloria gradually lifted Marie from the cabin floor. The Wolf was the first to speak.

With a very sad expression he looked at Marie and said, "Precious lady, I'm so sorry we lost him; however we must leave this ship. Gloria has set the C-4 charges to go at 0700.

We have exactly three minutes to get off this ship . . . let's move out!

Marie shouted, "No, I'll stay with Chris!"

Doug looked directly at the Wolf and read his facial expression. Without saying another word to Marie he hit her on the chin and knocked her unconscious. She gently fell across his right shoulder and they headed for the upper deck and bow of the ship. The Wolf dove overboard and reached the anchor chain and untied the rubber boat.

Immediately Gloria recognized she needed to be in the water when Doug released Marie over the side of the ship, she too dove into the frigid water. The minute Marie slipped into the cold water she regained consciousness and Gloria helped her climb into the boat. Now the time element became a very important issue. The Lenora was due to be destroyed within two minutes.

The Wolf and Doug had the oars of the small boat in hand and they rowed out of harms way.

Simpson let out a faint cry for help. He was suffering from hypothermia and was shaking violently as they pulled him into the boat. Later he would not be able to remember his benefactors! At exactly 0700 hours the first charge exploded at mid-ship. Now the Lenora was at drift, the second charged followed at 0702 and the third explosion followed immediately.

The Lenora went down in one hundred and twenty-eight feet of water. The helicopter pilot circled once again. Since the visibility had improved, he could see they had injured aboard the rubber boat. As he headed toward Pillar Point, he radioed for local ambulance service out of Pillar Point. The Pilot's thoughtfulness in dealing with a local ambulance service would afford the Wolf and his team additional time to make their way ashore.

While rowing ashore, Gloria recognized Simpson was not going to make it without some help. She started mouth to mouth resuscitation, while Marie pulled her body on top of Simpson in an effort to provide body heat.

Doug looked over toward the Wolf, "You know, it's bad Simpson is having a severe problem staying alive. If only he knew, he has two of the best looking women in the state of Washington working on him and he doesn't have a clue!"

"Row . . . . Doug, your paddling is out of sync, the Wolf yelled.

The Seattle Harbor Patrol and Seattle authorities were late in their response, allowing the assault team time to deliver Simpson to the waiting ambulance. The assignment on the Lenora and the four drug cartels, plus the Horizon group was drawing to a close. The Wolf and his team were soon driving on Highway 112 on their way to Seattle.

Chapter 35

Baker Hotel, Seattle Washington.

The Wolf was in his temporary lair, room # 1016. He had just finished talking with the Attorney General's staff representative, when he heard a gentle knock on the door. As he peered through the door peep hole he saw Gloria standing there with a gentle smile on her face. He quickly opened the door, pulling her toward him, he gently kissed her. From his perspective, it truly had been a long time since he had felt this way.

After the kiss, Gloria said, "Major Abbott, what'cha got cooking?"

"Absolutely nothing, I'm all yours."

"Excellent, let's keep it that way. I have someone in the hotel coffee shop I want you to meet."

"I look grungy; who is this mystery person?"

"Hopefully, your future brother-in-law!"

"What? Are you serious? Are you suggesting the possibility of marriage?"

"You are full of questions, aren't you? Which one do you want me to answer first?"

"The last one will do!"

"Let's go meet brother." The couple walked arm in arm to the elevator.

When the elevator doors opened Marie and Doug stepped out. They had come to the Brown Hotel to say goodbye, as they were about to leave for Chicago.

Doug spoke first, "Good morning you love birds. We wanted to say goodbye and to congratulate you on a job well done. We have a flight for Chicago which leaves in one hour, so we only have a moment.

Marie asked, "Do you need anything else from us before we catch the flight?"

Smiling, the Wolf said, "No not at this time. You both did one helluva job. Thanks for covering my rear-end. One question though, what did you do with Simpson?"

With a big grin, Doug replied, "Well, the doctors at Seattle General tell us he is going to be okay. He has had a lapse of memory; presently he does not remember any of us. The hospital has been in touch with his boss, Captain Turner. Turner will send a care flight to pick him up and deliver him to Cook Hospital in Chicago."

The Wolf said, "When he recovers I'll send him a note thanking him for handling Arthur Valdez. I'll always remember Simpson swings a mean ax! Oh, one other item. You both will be receiving a large check in the mail. Again, thanks and I'll be in touch soon."

The four hugged and said their goodbyes. The Wolf and Gloria headed for the coffee shop.

As they approached the doors to the coffee shop, the Wolf asked, "Is there anything special I need to know about brother?"

"He's the only family member I have left. Dad and Mom have been gone for some time.

She leaned over and kissed the Wolf on the cheek, I hope you like him."

As they approached brother's table he stood up, all six feet-five inches of him. He was wearing a gray pin-stripped business suit, with a solid black tie. The Wolf noticed he was a very distinguished looking individual with chiseled facial features, dark brown eyes, and graying in his hair. A quick assessment, he'd probably make a good brother-in-law!

"Major Jack Abbott, I would like for you to meet my brother, James Hampton."

"Major Abbott, the pleasure is mine. For the last couple of days all I've heard is Jack did this, and Jack did that! I'm real pleased to meet you and to know you are for real."

Smiling, Abbott returned the greeting, "It is good to meet you. One of the first comments Gloria made to me was about you. I was waiting for her at the airport when you had her paged."

"Yes, I thought she was coming in on a commercial flight. I should realize my sister has government support in her travels."

Gloria interrupted, "Jack, James is a Counselor at Law here in Seattle. He also is a new-born Christian and on occasion serves as a Gospel Minister. When Gloria finished her accolades, James Hampton handed Abbott his business card. The card reflected a law firm of Hampton, Pope, and Everett, LLP, Criminal Law Specialist!

Smiling Gloria said, "I just wanted you to know where you could find a good Criminal Attorney or a Minister if you ever needed one!"

Abbott looking directly at James Hampton said, "This information could come in handy in a short while!"

Gloria with a very serious look commented, "I've been waiting until we were all together to bring you both up to date. I have received orders via telephone to report to USMC Headquarters, Quantico, VA. day after tomorrow. It seems my services are needed in Iraq."

James was the first to respond, "Gloria, for how long?"

"I won't know until I receive my official orders at Quantico."

Looking downcast, Abbott said, "Let me talk to the Attorney General. I still need your expertise in this drug war."

"Jack, that's thoughtful of you to get involved. I have only six months left on this enlistment period. I've been thinking of 'hanging 'em up' for some time. Let me see what develops when I report for duty."

James Hampton easily read Jack Abbott's reaction to the news. He could tell he did not like what he heard. Jack seem to realize Gloria was about to be put in harms way once again!

After briefly discussing the overall situation, the group decided to share a brunch since it was late morning. James Hampton was very thoughtful in talking about Gloria's past and about their family. The conversation made Jack Abbott very comfortable in a family setting.

Time passed very rapidly as each participate was becoming more and more comfortable in each others company. James Hampton, looking at his watch wrinkled his brow.

James pushed his chair back from the table. "I'm so sorry I have to scoot. I have to be at the court house in an hour for a trial. It will take that long since I have to go by the office and pick up some paper work. Jack how long will you remain in Seattle?"

"Since Gloria is leaving, I'll stay and watch the Regatta. I need to grade the fall-out on this assignment.

I'm really concerned it will spill over into an international situation."

Smiling, James said, "Listen since you are staying over, the wife and family would like for you to stay with us. Why don't you check out of the Brown Hotel and I'll pick you up at 6:00 pm. I guess I should refer to that in military time . . . 1800 hours? I remember I always have trouble with Gloria on using the correct time. How about it?"

Gloria spoke up, "Darling, please say yes. You'll enjoy meeting Virginia and the kids. You'll have a great time!"

"James, I'm honored. I'll be at curbside at 1800 hours."

"Great!" James replied, "Oh, one other thing, I'm somewhat embarrassed to ask. Would you happen to have a couple of those 'silver wolf signets'? I'll pass them to my law partners. I have to be honest, they too have been keeping up with your accomplishments. Trust me, this is all on a confidential basis."

Jack Abbott reached in his pocket and handed three silver wolf signets to James. Hampton excused himself, while Gloria and Jack made future plans.

During their planning process they both agreed a lot depended on Gloria's Iraq transfer. If the transfer was only related to administrative services, Jack Abbott would stay stateside. If on the other hand, she would be used in recon or some front line sector, he would make active his oil and gas company operation. He felt very confident he could utilize the International Oil and Gas Company operation in the immediate Baghdad region.

The two mature adults were fascinated with each other and their love for each other seemed to be growing with leaps and bounds. Each one looked at their watches as the sun was setting and knew in a short while they would be parting.

While holding Gloria's hand, he suggested they freshen up for a dinner date and dancing before they told each other goodbye. Jack Abbott would come calling at exactly 1900 hours.

They both chuckled at the military time established.

Back in room #1016, Jack made an emergency cell phone call to Helen Schroeder. Helen answered her cell phone on the second beep.

"Schroeder here."

"Hey, where are you? I'm at Denver International Airport. What's going on?

"Would it be possible for you to stay in Denver for a couple of days?"

"Yes, I can arrange that. Dave Snider will continue on to the Chicago area. May I asked why you are coming to Denver?"

"I need to re-activate International Oil & Gas." I'll call you when I arrive at the airport."

Chapter 36

Denver, Colorado's . . . 1840 Hours.

When Jack Abbott arrived at Denver International Airport. He immediately called Helen Schroeder. Helen picked up her cell phone on the second ring. "I hope it's you since I don't talk to strangers," Helen said light-heartedly.

Jack was quick to comment. "As usual I like your promptness. Where are you located?"

"I am presently seated in the executive chair at International Oil and Gas. This place was a mess. You do realize you are not a very tidy person, don't you?".

Jack responded, "Okay, I'm going to start referring to you as my director of maintenance. I should be at the office by 1930 hours. Have you had dinner?"

"Not yet. Will you take me to the Alpine Restaurant? Best I recall that's where boy meets girl. Isn't that where you met the beautiful creature, Kathy McBride who had intent of doing you bodily harm?"

"Don't you ever forget?"

"No! I did not want to kill the good looking assassin, but desperate people do desperate things. Anyway, tell the taxi driver to hurry, I'm hungry."

The taxi made slow progress as a heavy snow began to fall; however, visibility was good as the marquees along Colorado Boulevard reflected red, green, and white lights along the way.

As the taxi drove up in front of the Page building, he saw Helen standing in the entry way talking with a man. Jack had the taxi driver stay on station while he walked to meet Helen.

As he neared the front doors he recognized James Ivey, the Page building superintendent. It was extremely important he be cordial and make comments which would leave Ivey thinking he and Helen were leaving town immediately.

Jack commented, "Well, Mr. Ivey it's been some time since our paths have crossed. How are you and the Page building tenants getting along?"

"It's good seeing you, Mr. Scoggins. Most of the tenants are doing okay. I still have one or two of the ladies who fuss over clogged toilets. For the most part, we're doing okay. I was just telling Miss Duvall all the guys around here have sure been missing her."

"Ivey, I hate to break the bad news. Miss Duvall and I are leaving for Iraq first thing tomorrow morning. We've just landed a huge drilling sub-contract with a major oil company. We'll probably be in Iraq for at least six months. Do you think you could keep an eye on our office for that length of time?"

"You bet, Mr. Scoggins, you can consider it a done deal," as he accepted one hundred dollars from Scoggins. Helen Schroeder could hardly hold back the laughter as they entered the taxi. Helen said. "Okay, sometimes I can read you like a book, but not tonight. What's going on?"

Smiling, Jack said, "I'll tell you over steaks, medium well, best I remember."

The Alpine Restaurant was still a busy place. When Jack requested a table near the back, the hostess seatcd them near where he had met Kathy McBride, the assassin.

Helen looking inquisitive asked, "Does this area look familiar to you?"

Smiling, Jack responded, "Sure does! If I could talk you into bleaching your hair blonde we'd be in business."

"I don't know why I went there. I deserved that comeback," Helen replied.

The two suddenly remained quite until after their food orders were placed. Jack smiling, opened the conversation.

With a solemn look on his face, "Helen, I apologize. I should not be so curt with you. I've got a lot on my mind and it's time to share with you," Jack explained.

With a slight frown on her face, Helen asked. "Is it about Gloria?"

"Yes, it's about both of us. Gloria had to report to Quantico, VA. It appears she will be transferred to Iraq. This is the reason I want to re-activate International Oil and Gas. I want to go to Iraq!"

Helen leaned back in her chair as in somewhat a state of shock. "Wow, I knew you were infatuated with her, but I didn't realize the love bug had bitten you this hard!"

"Yes, she's the only woman I have really cared about since I lost Connie.

"Of course, I care about you in a platonic way and have great respect for you. What I'm trying to say is, I have always looked upon you as a dear friend or relative. Maybe it was because of Steve Hightower, I'm really not sure. Of course, there have been times I have been attracted to you sexually, but I always put that feeling aside. I hope you understand what I'm saying."

While holding back tears and holding a stiff upper lip, Helen responded. "Jack, you fool.

You didn't owe me an explanation. I, have had special feelings for you. I know of the pain you have gone through over the years. I know you loved your family very much and I was afraid to try to replace them. It would have been wrong for me to try. I respect you very much and always will. Strange as it may seem, I like Gloria and I'm very pleased you have found someone to love. I also want you to know, I will be by your and Gloria's side all the way. Now, let's get down to business.

"Someone has been messing around in our office. All the bills have been picked up from the door drop area and placed on the desk. I started to ask Ivey if he knew anything about the mail being moved, but I didn't have time. It also appears someone had been pacing around the room. I saw foot prints on the floor. I think they need to change the air conditioning filters in the building to eliminate a lot of the dust. Long story made shorter, I cleaned the place up. The place looks pretty good now."

Smiling, Jack responded, "There you go again, taking care of what matters!"

The two executives of International Oil and Gas were in luck as they returned to the Page building. Mr. Ivey had called it a day and the entire building was empty except the guard on duty.

As they entered the lobby area, the guard stood up to greet them.

"Good evening, Miss Duvall. How's your evening going?"

"Jake, this has been a great evening so far. Do you remember Mr. Scoggins?"

"No maam, I've heard the name several times, and I know he is listed on my security check list."

Smiling, Helen said. "Jake, meet the man himself."

Jack with a friendly smile extended his hand. Both men returned greetings and it seemed security was satisfied. Jack and Helen moved rapidly to the elevators. They needed to pick up passports and other important papers for Jack's journey to Iraq. When they entered the elevator, Jake picked up the phone and called police headquarters.

Jake dialed Lt. James Harvel's phone extension direct. Since Harvel did not pick up, he left a short message, "Your man Scoggins is back in town!"

As Jack and Helen exited the elevators on the fourth floor, Jack pulled Helen close to him.

In a very low voice said, "We need to pick up the papers quickly, and get the hell out of Dodge! I think our friend Jake is on the take with the local authorities."

Helen asked, "How can you tell things like that?"

"He had shifty eye movement. I watched him closely as he kept reviewing his security list.

I believe it was flagged to call Police Headquarters in the event of my arrival. It's just a hunch, but it is a strong one!"

During the packing of important documents, Jack's cell phone rang. When he opened it he saw the call was from the Attorney Generals office, A-2. Jack answered his phone immediately.

"Wolf here."

Attorney General's Administrative Assistant said,. "The AG wants to meet with you in Washington, D.C. day after tomorrow at 0900 hours."

The Wolf answered, "Affirmative."

Helen asked, "What was that all about?"

Looking somewhat puzzled, The Wolf said, "I don't know. It has to be important; the assistant had no time for small talk."

Helen finished packing new I.D.'s, passports, and new Driver License for the Wolf. In all appearances his credentials would be in the name of Andrew Scoggins, Executive Officer for International Oil and Gas. As they turned out the office lights they heard a siren in the distance. It was time to clear the Page building. The Willow Inn motel was one block south on Colorado Boulevard. The two decided to rent rooms for the night. The following day, Jack Abbott would book passage to Washington, D.C. and Helen would return to Chicago.

Chapter 37

Washington, D.C., 0900.

When Major Jack Abbott walked into the Attorney General's office, the honorable John Tatum greeted him as though they were long lost brothers. Glancing around the room, Abbott noticed four other dignitaries seated around Tatum's desk. They too showed Abbott courtesy by standing up. It didn't take long for Abbott to realize this was no ordinary called meeting . . . this one was special. Taking a second glance around the room, he recognized the Secretary of State!

For the first time, he could tell the Attorney General was in deep trouble concerning something to do with his actions out in Seattle.

Tatum begin to speak, "Gentlemen, I called you all together so you will fully understand the arrangements I made with Major Abbott, aka, the Wolf. As each of you are aware our country has been attacked from outside and within. There's not a one of you in this room today who does not recognize the seriousness of our situation!

"In the beginning, I personally picked Major Abbott to help us clean up the drug and related problems. I felt he was the best qualified to conduct a covert operation! Since the initial assignment, the work has grown by leaps and bounds. As a matter of fact, it has grown so large it was necessary for me to assign one of our top Marines from G-2, First Marine Division to assist in the last endeavor. The Marine is Colonel Gloria Hampton.

"I just received word this morning from the Marine Corp Commandant, she has notified her department she intends to retire in six months. Looking directly at Jack Abbott, Tatum could not help but notice the silly grin on Jack's face. Abbott would you know anything about that?"

"Yes sir, I heard the same thing." The Secretary of State laughed along with the others.

"Gentlemen, I guess I'd best get back to our problems or opportunities at hand. What this amounts to is I've got my butt in big trouble. The Secretary of State informs me that Columbia, Spain, Mexico, and Cambodia are all up in arms about the killing of some of their people. Come to find out, a lot of the deceased have supported their country officials with cash derived from the drug Cartels. In essence, they are raising hell over nothing; yet, my office is feeling the heat from our President. Down to the bottom line, it seems we have to get along with these low-life bastards!

Major Abbott, at this very hour I must rescind my commission to you. You will discontinue every effort to dismantle the drug cartels and their related operations. I personally want you to know it hurts me to issue this order! Before these witnesses today, my department is granting you $1,000,000 in tax free currency. In this case you may consider it a salary or a bonus for doing one helluva job for your country! The Attorney General handed Abbott a manila envelop. Winking he said, "By the way, I hope you and the Marine Corp Colonel, will settle down on a turkey farm somewhere in Texas!"

The meeting was adjourned.

Jack Abbott was one happy man. He actually felt as though he had dodged a bullet. The special meeting with the Attorney General could have gone badly. After all, he had broken laws of the land on both national and international levels and he realized it at the time of occurrence.

To know the laws and blatantly disobey them is a no-no!

Abbott was fortunate the Attorney General was not looking for a scape goat. Had he been wanting to go that route, he had Major Jack Abbott in his cross hairs. It became apparent the current government administration had decided to sanction the attacks on the drug cartels because of the vast amounts of money involved. In this situation, there were two major positions for consideration. First, the money retrieved on cartel raids would be immediately credited to the US Treasury. Secondly, by eliminating the cartels function, the cost for maintaining surveillance and police actions by federal and local enforcement agencies would be significantly reduced.

For whatever reason, he was off the hook and most thankful. As he walked down the steps of the federal building, he opened his cell phone and it was a call from Colonel Hampton.

Her voice sounded crisp and fresh, "Good morning, Major. Is it a morning for you to howl?"

"Good morning to you precious lady, may we talk about the marriage proposal you recently presented to me?"

"Major have you accepted?"

"I'm thinking about it. By the way, I don't have a job anymore, I've been fired!

Gloria with a perky sounding voice, "I knew the minute they found out we had been fraternizing, one of us would have to go!"

"What are you talking about?"

Still sounding excited, Gloria responded, "Well, when I told the Commandant I was not going to re-up for another tour of duty, he asked me why. I just went ahead and told him I had an affair with a Marine Corp Major!"

"You didn't."

"You bet I did! Once I fell in love, I decided to tell the whole world."

Abbott finally come to realize Gloria was putting him together. The interesting part was he was enjoying every minute of it. Then he asked a very pertinent question, "Darling, I need you to answer this important question. How would you enjoy turkey farming in South Texas?"

Gloria thought for a moment, "You know great minds run in the same channel. The Commandant recommended I start raising turkeys in Texas when I retire from the Corp!"

Abbott responded, "You're crazy, but I love you. Have you received your assignment to Iraq?"

Laughing, Gloria said, "I knew there was some reason I called you. I'm staying stateside. My commanding officer said he did not want to transfer me since I've been acting goofy. He said I would mess-up 1st Marine Reconnaissance Company. I need you!"

Just the sound of Gloria's voice was enough to make him think all was well with the world. Quick came Jack's reply, "I need you too. Are you staying on base or have you located a condo as yet?"

"I'm still in base housing. I've looked at several condos and apartments but have not made a decision. Are you coming to Virginia?"

"Yes, I'm catching a shuttle flight this afternoon. I'll meet you at Marine Headquarters, front gate at 1900 hours. I need a good attorney, so I think I'll call James Hampton out in Seattle. Do you think that would be a good idea?"

Gloria raised her voice, "Oh, I was afraid if I left you alone you would get into trouble!"

Jack's response was quick, "Darling, you are the trouble. All I think about is being with you. When I arrive in Virginia you must be ready with a 'yes' or 'no'. Do you feel you can handle that?"

Gloria's voice level changed to a sexy whisper, "Thank goodness, I have a few hours to think about the question. Please catch an earlier flight."

Jack sounded all business like, "I suggest you wear you're shopping shoes as part of your evening attire, bye."

On the short shuttle flight, Jack inquired about top rated jewelry firms within the area. After the greetings, he would suggest a quick shopping tour for an engagement ring. All systems go!

When Gloria saw Jack standing by the waiting taxi, she burst into tears. As they embraced, Jack also became emotional because he realized he had life anew. His life had much more meaning, and he prayed his killing days were over.

Holding Gloria in his arms he asked, "Will you marry me?"

Gloria pressed against him, "Yes, yes, and yes. As you know I'm noted for a lady of very few words, but I just want to make sure you heard me!"

Jack stepped back from the embrace and peered down at Gloria's shoes. The lady had on low heels, she was dressed for shopping." Jack Abbott directed the taxi to Goldberg's fine jewelry store.

En-route he asked Gloria if it would be appropriate to ask her brother, James Hampton, for her hand in marriage. Gloria responded by saying it was not absolutely necessary; however, it would be a nice gesture, and James would be appreciative.

Jack inquired, "Do you have him programmed in your cell phone call list?"

"I do and I'll activate for you." She made the call and James answered immediately.

"Hello Colonel, what's happening? Are you calling from Iraq?"

Gloria replied, "Hello brother, I'll calling you from Virginia and I have a fellow Marine who would like to speak to you."

"Good, put the man on. I've been expecting to hear from him!"

Smiling big, Jack said, "Good morning, I'm calling you because I need a good attorney.

I've met this good looking woman by the name of Gloria. I would appreciate you drafting a per-nuptial agreement stating everything she has of material value will belong to me if I marry her! This agreement should be made ready within six months. Will your law firm be able to handle this without being prejudiced?" Without hearing her brother's reply, Gloria was laughing out loud.

James Hampton, Attorney at Law could not keep from chuckling himself. Finally he regained his composure. "Mr. Abbott, I'll call my associates together to discuss this matter as the outcome will probably be decided by vote. However, prior to me presenting this to the entire law firm, I would like to know for sure you have decided to marry this wild woman, have you? If the answer is 'yes', then you certainly have my blessing. I might be quick to add you also have my deepest sympathy!"

Jack was smiling as though he had hit a huge jackpot in Las Vegas, "James, thank you very much. Of course, I'm most grateful that I soon will be a part of your family. Your sister wants to talk to you. I look forward to seeing you and Virginia and the kids in the near future."

Laughing Gloria said, "Brother thanks for giving me away. Jack and I have not discussed location for our marriage ceremony, but it would be nice to be married at your estate.

Would that be permissible?"

"Absolutely, Virginia and the kids will be thrilled to hear this news. Love you."

Chapter 38

Vasho Island, Washington . . . .
Six months later.

The wedding was the talk of Vasho Island, and took place on the estate of James and Virginia Hampton. An estate of twenty acres beautifully manicured, with flowers of the region and accented by tall northern pine trees. A perfect setting for a very special couple. James Hampton did not miss a word as he had the couple recite their vows. Doug Snider served as Jack's best man and Helen Schroeder caught the bride's bouquet! The honeymoon would be spent traveling Canada, from the west coast to the east coast, after which the couple would establish residence on a ranch Jack Abbott had bought during their six month engagement period.

When Jack purchased the ranch it was named, "The Chaparral" and consisted of 22,000 acres. At the time of purchase, he changed the name of the ranch to, "Wolf Lair", and recorded the deed of trust in Gloria Hampton's name. The ranch was a beautiful spread situated ninety miles south of Alpine, Texas and three miles west of Highway 118. The land was bordered on the northeast by Turkey Peak and on the south by the San Jacinto mountain range . . . good horse country. The place had good water and the Concho river ran through it. In addition to raising thoroughbred Quarter Horses, the newly wed couple might try their hand at 'turkey raising', since some of their dear friends had suggested it! Their food staples, plus gas would be purchased at Henry and Martha's General Store, ten miles north on Highway 118. They were likable folks, truly a mom and pop store operation.

Southwest Texas.

The honeymoon over, both Jack and Gloria were beginning to adjust to ranch life and were enjoying every minute together. It seems ranch life was really satisfying, since each were putting on a little extra weight. In short order they had remodeled the stucco ranch house and shored up the ceiling areas with fresh cut pine timbers.

Gloria finished sweeping the large front porch and came in for a cold glass of tea. She looked toward the corral and noticed Jack was working with 'Stormy' a newly purchased stallion. As she watched the dust fly out of the corral, she had her doubts about whether or not Jack was able to handle the animal. Looking north over the corral fence she noticed three buckskin mares tied to a hitching post. Without finishing her tea she headed for the corral.

Leaning against the corral fence she yelled to Jack, "Darling, do you have a minute?"

"Sure, for a good-looking woman I'll take time."

"Jack, as you are aware I know very little about horses, but I think I can help you out with Stormy!"

"Woman, I love you too much to allow you in here with this wild bastard. He's tried to bite me three times. I've eared him down twice. He nearly kicked the fool out of me. No maam, I think it best you stay on that side of the corral fence."

"Tell you what, cowboy. Let's go to the porch and let me fix you a cold glass of ice tea and you and old Stormy rest for awhile. How about it?"

"That's the first reasonable thing you've said in the last five minutes," Jack replied.

Jack was enjoying the fresh southeast breeze and the glass of ice tea so much he forgot about Stormy. In the meanwhile, Gloria walked through the barn and went directly to the hitching post and untied the mares. She slowly walked them into the barn as Stormy let out a couple of soft snorts. She made her way back to the house without disturbing Jack.

Gloria asked,"Darling, how about a refill on the ice tea?"

Aroused and smiling, "No thanks, I've got to take care of that Stallion and see if I can calm him down a bit. It's for sure I can't throw a saddle on him the way he's acting up."

Smiling Gloria asked, "Am I allowed to come and watch?"

"Yeah, sure thing as long as you stay out of the corral."

When Jack crawled over the coral fence, Stormy was slowly walking in a circle around the fence. On occasion he would let out a gentle snort and peer toward the barn.

Jack looking directly at Stormy, "Okay wild one come to daddy."

Jack gently placed a rope around his neck and led him to the hitching post. Pulling a saddle blanket and saddle off the fence he slowly placed it on the horse's back. Stormy just looked back at him and nudged him with his nose.

Jack looking over the corral fence at Gloria said, "Can you beat that. This sucker didn't even have a glass of ice tea. What do you think came over him?"

Gloria grinning, "Darling, I would say it's a case of 'out of sight, out of mind'!

"Hell, that's not it. I wasn't gone that long," Jack retorted.

"Darling, you're doing a good job. If it's okay with you, I think I'll drive in to Henry and Martha's General Store and pick-up some food items. I might even buy you some of your favorite ice cream. I'll be back in a couple of hours, okay?"

"Sounds like a deal to me. Be sure and take the 12 gauge shotgun with you. You may see a rattler before you come to Highway 118. Be sure and take your cell phone. I love you, be careful!"

By this time Jack was sitting atop Stormy circling the corral. He watched Gloria's vehicle kicking up dust until she was out of sight.

After three miles of driving over rough gravel roads, Gloria reached Highway 118 and turned north toward Henry and Martha's General Store. She had driven two miles and she noticed a black pickup truck approaching from the rear.

Absolutely no doubt in her mind, whoever was driving was exceeding the sixty mile an hour speed limit. As the pickup drew closer she observed the unit was a Dodge Ram Club pickup, with four male passengers, two in the front seat and two in the back seat. Gloria quickly recognized they where male Caucasians, ranging in age from forty to late twenties. Since their vehicle was weaving down the highway, she determined they had probably been drinking.

As they pulled along side her vehicle, one of the older males yelled. "Hey pretty woman we need to talk to you!"

Gloria tried to ignore the four men, as she accelerated her vehicle and looked straight ahead.

Again, the men pulled along side, "Lady, you are about to have a blow-out. Your left rear tire is very low. Pull over and we will help you change the tire," Gloria continued to ignore the men. She had slowed down to fifty-five miles an hour. She picked up her cell and called Jack. Jack answered his cell phone immediately.

In a rushed voice, Gloria said, "Darling I'm about three miles north on Highway 118, I have four men in a black dodge pickup harassing me. Can you come quickly?"

"Do you have the shotgun?"

"Yes, I loaded it with five rounds of buckshot!"

"I'm on my way. Do your best to make it to the General Store. I'll catch up!"

Gloria continued driving straight ahead. The terrain in front of her was level and she could see the black pickup approximately six hundred yards in front of her. Suddenly the pickup stopped and pulled across the highway, leaving only the bar ditches as avenues to pass. Gloria had no doubt whatsoever these men meant her harm. She reached over and pulled the shotgun close to her. The double-barrel shotgun would do severe damage at close range. She slowed her vehicle speed to thirty miles an hour as she entered the right bar ditch. In the ditch she again slowed her speed to ten miles an hour. When she re-entered Highway 118 she was sixty feet from the black pickup. She spun her vehicle around to face the four men! By this time the four men were standing near the front of their vehicle.

Gloria stepped out of her vehicle and pulled the shotgun up to her right shoulder.

She yelled, "Men you need to know, I have buckshot in the weapon. I can cut you in half. Stop your pursuit!"

One of the older men, the driver yelled back. "You bitch, we just want to show you a good time."

Gloria answered, "Let me show you one". She fired the right side barrel of the twelve gauge hitting right rear panel of their truck. The four men hurried to get inside the truck and sped off, south bound on Highway 118. Gloria watched the pickup until it was out of sight.

She called Jack and brought him up to date. He had just reached Highway 118.

"Darling, continue driving on to the store. I'll probably be about five minutes behind you, providing this old jeep doesn't quit on me."

"Thanks for watching my back. I'll see you at the store and I'll buy you a soda-pop!"

Traveling north on Highway 118, Jack kept checking every vehicle he passed. He was looking for a black pickup with buck shot damage to the right rear panel. When he arrived at the store, he saw Gloria's vehicle parked on the south side of the building. He pulled his jeep along side. He entered the front of the store and greeted Henry. While Martha was waiting on another customer, he looked around for Gloria but she was out of sight. Henry motioned to Jack she was in the lady's room.

Jack smiling, "Good morning Henry, how's it going?"

With a frown on his face he looked directly at Jack, "Well, it was going good until the McCright boys came in and bought four six packs of Schlitz beer! Damn they are rough when they are drinking. A couple of them have already been in prison for molesting a school teacher. When the older brother, Jess McCright, is on the loose they become dangerous! They live about twenty miles north of here. When they come in the store, I have Martha go to the house because they become real rowdy and no telling what they might say or do."

Just as Henry had uttered his last sentence, the McCright's drove up front for gas.

Henry looked at Jack, "Here we go again, the bastards are back for fuel."

Jack smiling, "Tell you what Henry, I'm you're new employee, so let me pump the gas, okay?"

Henry looked astonished! "Yeah, that will be okay. Please don't make Jess McCright upset; he will wreck this place."

With a bigger smile on his face, Jack said, "Henry, absolutely no problem."

Just as Jack stepped out front to serve Henry's special customers, Gloria emerged from the ladies room. Martha's customer left out as Jack was greeting the McCright's.

When Jack walked up to the driver's side of the pickup, he saw where Gloria's shot had hit the rear panel. By the time Jack had reached the driver's door, Jess McCright stepped out from behind the wheel. He was a large man, unshaven and smelled as though he hadn't had a bath in some time. One of the younger McCright's walked around the front of the pickup and approached Jess.

"Jess, did you see what I saw when we drove in?"

"What the hell are you talking about, Andy?"

"I'm talking about the bitche's car. You know the one who shot our pickup?"

Jess smiling, said. "You've got to be kidding me. Where is she?"

Andy replied, "I'm guessing she's inside. We'll go get her!"

"Hell, I'll go with you. I owe that lady something!"

Jack Abbott had been privileged to hear all of their conversation. He quickly viewed the situation as being serious. The way he had it figured, somebody was going to be hurt, and he did not want it to be Gloria, Henry, or Martha. He greeted his adversaries!

"Good morning, what can I do for you this morning?"

Jess looking directly at Jack Abbott, "And who in the hell are you?"

"Oh, I'm Henry's new hire. I attend to all the front traffic. You know like pumping gas, sweeping out the floorboards, emptying ash trays, fixing tires. You know that kind of work."

Frowning, Jess said. "Fill it up, while we go inside and see a bitch!"

"Sure thing. I'll give you full service in a couple of minutes."

As the McCright's headed for the front door of the store, Jack headed for his jeep.

From underneath the front seat he pulled out a hickory hatchet handle, he had recently bought at a lumber yard. He placed the hatchet handle under his belt and headed for the store to face the McCright's.

When he entered the store, Jess McCright had Gloria by the hair and had her bent over the front counter. Andy was helping hold her, while the two younger McCright's had Henry and Martha backed up against the candy counter.

Jack had the hatchet handle concealed behind his back. He said in a calm voice, "Mr. McCright I have your pickup serviced."

Laughing, Jess said, "You idiot, can't you see I'm busy? I'm about to teach this bitch a lesson!

"Yes sir, I sure see that. When I met you out front I failed to mention the other services, I provide for Henry and Martha. I suggest you turn the lady loose!"

Jess, looking at his two younger brothers near the candy counter yelled, "Get him!"

As the two bothers ran toward him, Jack turned over a potato chip stand in front of them.

When the first one managed to gain his footing, Jack thrust the hatchet handle into his thorax. He grabbed his throat and went down. As the second man pulled himself off the floor, Jack spun in front of him and placed his right foot to the left side of his head. The kick was fast and hard knocking the man through the front glass window into the service area. With the fast maneuvers, he had managed to get Jess and Andy's attention!

Andy immediately released his hold on Gloria and ran out the front door. Jess backed up and looked at Jack and asked again. "Who are you?"

Smiling, Jack said. "Jess, you were so rude in the beginning you didn't give me a chance to tell you. To make a long story short, I teach big ugly men like you how to be nice and polite to ladies! It's lesson time. I'm going to give you and your brothers the opportunity to apologize to these ladies; or, you each will have to face the consequences."

Jess was not sober enough to heed the warning! "Mister, you're messing with the wrong McCright. I'll do the teaching here today."

Jess made one big mistake as he pulled a hunting knife and lunged forward toward Jack!

Jack went into a defensive stance positioning the hatchet handle, wherein he could slap or punch with the weapon. He parred Jess's knife thrust and brought the hatchet handle across the bridge of Jess's nose, crushing the bone. Jess backed up and let out a loud cry in pain. The second blow came across Jess's right forearm breaking bones just above his right hand. Jess dropped the knife and ran toward his pickup. By this time Andy McCright felt he should help Jess, he grabbed a hammer out of the back of their pickup and swung at Jack. Jack side stepped the blow and punched with the hatchet handle, breaking three ribs on his right side. Suddenly, all of the McCright's ran for their pickup and sped off without paying for the gas.

Jack ran to Gloria to find she was comforting Martha. Henry put his arm around Jack while thanking him for a job well done.

Smiling, Henry said, "I've witnessed a lot in my life time, but I have never seen a combat performance like this. Looking at Jack, "Please take whatever groceries you need, you have certainly earned a great deal."

Jack commented, "Henry, we appreciate your kind offer, but we'll continue our shopping and pay you for the staples we need. We just want to be good neighbors and live in peace.

I believe the McCright's have learned a lesson today. Hopefully, you will not have anymore problems with them. We just appreciate the opportunity to help you."

Arriving back at the Wolf's Lair ranch, Jack looking at Gloria, "Darling, I'm so glad the killing is behind us, and we will be able to live in peace."

Gloria hugged her husband and whispered, "I'm so proud of you!"

The sun was setting over Wolf's Lair, so the newly weds moved out on the front porch to enjoy the southeast breeze. As they were relaxing in the porch swing, they begin to reminisce as to how they met.

"Mr. Abbott, I have a confession to make. I wanted you the first time I laid eyes on you!"

Jack with a slight grin asked, "Why didn't you take me? You know I'm easy!"

Gloria retorted, "Abbott, ladies don't do that, and I'm very much a lady."

"Yes maam, you surely are. Let's go make love, western style."

Gloria pulled back in the swing and asked, "What's western style?"

"Beautiful lady, it's one of those deals I have to show you. It's just not possible to explain.

Come follow me!"

"Darling, before we go inside I have one very important question, "Can we have a baby?"

Jack's expression changed, "Do you want to have a baby?"

Gloria drew close and held up four fingers! Jack pulled her close and gently kissed her.

It was 0400 when Jack's cell phone rang. On the first series of rings Jack did not answer the phone. It was exactly fifteen minutes later his phone rang again. This time Jack opened the phone and peered at the screen. AG-1 appeared in red. It was an urgent message. This time it was not oral, it was a text message and it read, "New Assignment . . . Yemen, Semper Fidelis!"